THE GOVERNESS

AND OTHER STORIES

STEFAN ZWEIG

THE GOVERNESS

AND OTHER STORIES

Translated from the German by
Anthea Bell

PUSHKIN PRESS
LONDON

Original texts © Williams Verlag
English translations © Anthea Bell 2011

Did He Do It? first published in German as
War er es? (between 1935 and 1940)

The Miracles of Life first published in German as
Die Wunder des Lebens (1903)

Downfall of the Heart first published in German as
Untergang eines Herzens (1927)

The Governess first published in German as
Die Gouvernante (1907)

This edition first published in 2011 by

Pushkin Press
12 Chester Terrace
London NW1 4ND

ISBN 978 1 906548 35 3

Cover Illustration: *On the Hillside* 1914 Heinrich Kuhn
© Österreichische Nationalbibliothek Vienna
Frontispiece: *Stefan Zweig*
© Roger-Viollet Rex Features

Set in 10.5 on 13 Monotype Baskerville
by Alma Books Limited
and printed in Great Britain on Munken Premium White 90 gsm
by TJ International Ltd, Padstow, Cornwall

www.pushkinpress.com

CONTENTS

THE GOVERNESS

AND OTHER STORIES

DID HE DO IT?

PERSONALLY I'M AS GOOD as certain that he was the murderer. But I don't have the final, incontrovertible proof. "Betsy," my husband always tells me, "you're a clever woman, a quick observer, and you have a sharp eye, but you let your temperament lead you astray, and then you make up your mind too hastily." Well, my husband has known me for thirty-two years, and perhaps, indeed probably, he's right to warn me against forming a judgement in too much of a hurry. So as there is no conclusive evidence, I have to make myself suppress my suspicions, especially in front of other people. But whenever I meet him, whenever he comes over to me in that forthright, friendly way of his, my heart misses a beat. And a little voice inside me says: he and no one else was the murderer.

So I am going to try reconstructing the entire course of events again, just for my own satisfaction.

About six years ago my husband had come to the end of his term of service as a distinguished government official in the colonies, and we decided to retire to some quiet place in the English countryside, to spend the rest of our days, already approaching their evening, with such pleasures of life as flowers and books. Our choice was a small village in the country near Bath.

A narrow, slowly flowing waterway, the Kennet and Avon Canal, winds its way from that ancient and venerable city, passing under many bridges, towards the valley of Limpley Stoke, which is always green. The canal was built with much skill and at great expense over a century ago, to carry coal from Cardiff to London, and has many wooden locks and lock-keepers' stations along its length. Horses moving at a ponderous trot on the narrow towpaths to right and left of the canal used to pull the broad, black barges along the wide waterway at a leisurely pace. It was planned and built on a generous scale, and was a good means of transport for an age when time still did not mean much. But then came the railway to bring the black freight to the capital city far more cheaply and easily. Canal traffic ground to a halt, the canal fell into decay and dilapidation, but the very fact that it is entirely deserted and serves no useful purpose makes it a romantic, enchanted place today. Waterweed grows so densely from the bottom of the sluggish, black water that the surface has a shimmer of dark green, like malachite; pale water lilies sway on the smooth surface of the canal, which reflects the flower-grown banks, the bridges and the clouds with photographic accuracy. There is barely a ripple moving on the drowsy waterway. Now and then, half sunk in the water and already overgrown with plants, a broken old boat by the bank recalls the canal's busy past, of which even the visitors who come to take the waters in

Bath hardly know anything, and when we two elderly folk walked on the level towpath where the horses used to pull barges laboriously along by ropes in the old days, we would meet no one for hours on end except, perhaps, pairs of lovers meeting in secret to protect, by coming to this remote place, their youthful happiness from neighbours' gossip, before it was officially declared by their engagement or marriage.

We were delighted by the quiet, romantic waterway set among rolling hills. We bought a plot of land in the middle of nowhere, just where the slope from Bathampton falls gently to the waterside as a beautiful, lush meadow. At the top of the rise we built a little country cottage, with a pleasant garden path leading past fruit trees, vegetable beds and flower beds and on down to the canal, so that when we sat out of doors on our little garden terrace beside the water we could see the meadow, the house and the garden reflected in the canal. The house was more peaceful and comfortable that anywhere I had ever dreamt of living, and my only complaint was that it was rather lonely, since we had no neighbours.

"Oh, they'll soon come when they see what a pretty place we've found to live in," said my husband, cheering me.

And sure enough; our little peach trees and plum trees had hardly established themselves in the garden before, one day, signs of another building going up next to our house suddenly appeared. First came busy estate agents, then surveyors, and after them builders and carpenters. Within a dozen or so weeks a little cottage with a red-tiled roof was nestling beside ours. Finally a removal van full of furniture arrived. We heard constant banging and hammering in the formerly quiet air, but we had not yet set eyes on our new neighbours.

One morning there was a knock at our door. A pretty, slender woman with clever, friendly eyes, not much more than twenty-eight or twenty-nine, introduced herself as our neighbour and asked if we could lend her a saw; the workmen had forgotten to bring one. We fell into conversation. She told us that her husband worked in a bank in Bristol, but for a long time they had both wanted to live somewhere more remote, outside the city, and as they were walking along the canal one Sunday they had fallen in love with the look of our house. Of course it would mean a journey of an hour each way for her husband from home to work and back, but he would be sure to find pleasant travelling companions and would easily get used to it. We returned her call next day. She was still on her own in the house, and told us cheerfully that her husband wouldn't be joining her until all the work was finished. She really couldn't do with having him underfoot until then, she said, and after all, there was no hurry. I don't know why, but I didn't quite like the casual way she spoke of her husband's absence, almost as if she were pleased not to have him there. When we were sitting over our meal alone at home,

I commented that she didn't appear to be very fond of him. My husband told me I shouldn't keep jumping to hasty conclusions; he had thought her a very agreeable young woman, intelligent and pleasant, and he hoped her husband would be the same.

And it wasn't long before we met him. As we were taking our usual evening walk one Saturday, when we had just left our house, we heard footsteps behind us, brisk and heavy, and when we turned we saw a large, cheerful-looking man catching up with us, offering us a large, red, freckled hand. He was our new neighbour, he said, he'd heard how kind we had been to his wife. Of course he ought not to be greeting us like this in his shirtsleeves, without paying a formal visit first. But his wife had told him so many nice things about us that he really couldn't wait a minute longer to thank us. So here he was, John Charleston Limpley by name, and wasn't it a famous thing—they'd already called the valley Limpley in his honour long before he himself could ever guess that he'd be looking for a house here some day? Yes, here he was, he said, and here he hoped to stay as long as the good Lord let him live. He liked this place better than anywhere else in the world, and he would promise us here and now, hand on his heart, to be a good neighbour.

He talked so fast and cheerfully, with such a flow of words, that you hardly had a chance to get a word in. So I at least had plenty of time to scrutinise him thoroughly. Limpley was a powerful figure of a man, at least six foot tall, with broad, square shoulders that would have graced a navvy, but he seemed to have a good-natured, childlike disposition, as giants so often do. His narrowed, slightly watery eyes twinkled confidently at you from between their reddish lids. As he talked and laughed, he kept showing his perfect white teeth. He didn't know quite what to do with his big, heavy hands, and had some difficulty in keeping them still. You felt that he would have liked to clap you on the shoulder in comradely fashion with those hands, and as if to work off some of his strength he at least cracked the joints of his fingers now and then.

Could he, he asked, join us on our walk, in his shirt-sleeves just as he was? When we said yes, he walked along with us talking nineteen to the dozen. He was of Scottish descent on his mother's side, he told us, but he had grown up in Canada. Now and then he pointed to a fine tree or an attractive slope; how beautiful, he said, how incomparably beautiful that was! He talked, he laughed, he expressed enthusiasm for everything almost without stopping. An invigorating current of strength and cheerfulness emanated from this large, healthy, vital man, infectiously carrying us away with it. When we finally parted, my husband and I both felt pleased with the warmth of his personality. "It's a long time since I met such a hearty, full-blooded fellow," said my husband who, as I have already indicated, is usually rather cautious and withdrawn in assessing character.

But it wasn't long before our first pleasure in finding such an agreeable new neighbour began to diminish considerably. There could not be the least objection to Limpley as a human being. He was good-natured to a fault, he was interested in others, and so anxious to be obliging that you were always having to decline his helpful offers. In addition he was a thoroughly decent man, modest, open and by no means stupid. But after a while it became difficult to put up with his effusive, noisy way of being permanently happy. His watery eyes were always beaming with contentment about anything and everything. All that he owned, all that he encountered was delightful, wonderful; his wife was the best woman in the world, his roses the finest roses, his pipe the best pipe ever seen, and he smoked the best tobacco in it. He could spend a full quarter-of-an-hour trying to convince my husband that a pipe ought to be filled just so, in exactly the way he filled his own, and that while his tobacco was a penny cheaper than more expensive brands it was even better. Always bubbling over as he was with excessive enthusiasm about the most unimportant, natural and indifferent of things, he evidently had an urge to expound the reasons for falling into such banal raptures at length. The noisy engine running inside him was never switched off. Limpley couldn't work in his garden without singing at the top of his voice, couldn't talk without laughing uproariously and gesticulating, couldn't read the paper without jumping up when he came upon a news item that aroused his interest and running round to tell us about it. His huge, freckled hands were always assertive, like his big heart. It wasn't just that he patted every horse and every dog he met; my husband had to put up with many a comradely and uninhibited Canadian slap on the knee when they sat comfortably talking together. Because his own warm, full heart, which constantly overflowed with emotion, took an interest in everything, he assumed that it was only natural for everyone else to take a similar interest, and you had to resort to all kinds of little tricks to ward off his insistent kindness. He respected no one's hours of rest or even sleep, because bursting as he was with health and strength he simply could not imagine anyone else ever feeling tired or downcast. You found yourself secretly wishing he would take a daily dose of bromide to lower his magnificent but near-intolerable vitality to a more normal level. Several times, when Limpley had spent an hour sitting with us—or rather not sitting, but leaping up and down and striding around—I caught my husband instinctively opening the window, as if the presence of that dynamic and somehow barbaric man had overheated the room. While you were with him, looking into his bright, kindly eyes—and they were indeed always brimming over with kindness—you couldn't dislike him. It was only later that you felt you were worn out and wished him at the Devil. Before we knew Limpley, we old folk had never guessed that such admirable qualities as kindness, goodness of heart, frankness and warmth of feeling could drive us to distraction in their obtrusive superfluity.

I now also understood what I had found incomprehensible at first, that it by no means showed lack of affection on his wife's part when she accepted his absence with such cheerful equanimity. For she was the real victim of his extravagant good humour. Of course he loved her passionately, just as he passionately loved everything that was his. It was touching to see him treat her so tenderly and with such care; she had only to cough once and he was off in search of a coat for her, or poking the fire to fan the flames, and if she went on an expedition to Bath he overwhelmed her with good advice as if she had to survive a dangerous journey. I never heard an unkind word pass between the two of them; on the contrary, he loved to sing her praises to the point where it became quite embarrassing. Even in front of us, he couldn't refrain from caressing her and stroking her hair, and above all enumerating her many beauties and virtues. "Have you noticed what pretty little fingernails my Ellen has?" he would suddenly ask, and in spite of her bashful protest he made her show us her hands. Then I was expected to admire the way she arranged her hair, and of course we had to taste every batch of jam she made, since in his opinion it was infinitely better than anything the most famous jam manufacturers of England could produce. Ellen, a quiet, modest woman, always sat with her eyes cast down on these embarrassing occasions, looking uncomfortable. She seemed to have given up defending herself against her husband's boisterous behaviour. She let him talk and tell stories and laugh, putting in only an occasional weary, "Oh, really?" or, "Fancy that."

"She doesn't have an easy life," commented my husband one day when we were going home. "But one can't really hold it against him. He's a good soul at heart, and she may well be happy with him."

"I'm not so sure about the happiness," I said rather sharply. "If you ask me, all that ostentatious happiness is too much to take—fancy making such a show of his feelings! I'd go mad living with so much excessive emotion. Don't you see that he's making his wife very *un*happy with all that effervescence and positively murderous vitality?"

"Oh, you're always exaggerating," said my husband, and I suppose he was right, really. Limpley's wife was by no means unhappy, or rather she wasn't even that any more. By now she was probably incapable of any pronounced feeling of her own; she was simply numbed and exhausted by Limpley's vast exuberance. When he went to his office in the morning, and his last cheery 'Goodbye' died away at the garden gate, I noticed that the first thing she did was to sit down or lie down for a little while without doing anything, just to enjoy the quiet atmosphere all around her. And there would be something slightly weary in her movements all day. It wasn't easy to get into conversation with her, for she had almost forgotten how to speak for herself in their eight years of marriage. Once she told me how they had met. She had been living with her parents in the country, he had strolled by on an outing, and in his wild way he had swept her off her feet; they were engaged and then married before she really knew what he was like or even what his profession was. A quiet, pleasant woman, she never said a word, not a syllable to suggest that she wasn't happy, and yet as a woman myself I sensed where the real crux of that marriage lay. In the first year they had taken it for granted that they would have a baby, and it was the same in the second and third years of their marriage. Then after six or seven years they had given up hope, and now her days were too empty, while her evenings were too full of his boisterous high spirits. It would be a good idea, I thought to myself, if she were to adopt a child, or take to some kind of sporting activity, or find a job. All that sitting around was bound to lead to melancholy, and melancholy in turn to a kind of hatred for his provoking cheerfulness, which was certainly likely to exhaust any normal person. She ought to have someone, anyone with her, or the tension would be too strong.

As chance would have it, I had owed an old friend of my youth who lived in Bath a visit for weeks. We had a comfortable chat, and then she suddenly remembered that she wanted to show me something charming, and took me out into the yard. At first all I could see in the dim light of a shed was a group of small creatures of some kind tumbling about in the straw, crawling over each other and mock-fighting. They were four bulldog puppies of six or seven weeks old, stumbling about on their big paws, now and then trying to utter a little squeal of a bark. They were indeed charming as they staggered out of the basket where their mother lay, looking massive and suspicious. I picked one of them up by his profuse white coat. The puppy was brown and white, and with his pretty snub nose he did credit to his distinguished pedigree, as his mistress explained to me. I couldn't refrain from playing with him, teasing him and getting him excited so that he snapped clumsily at my fingers. My friend asked if I would like to take him home with me; she loved the puppies very much, she said, and she was ready to give them away if she could be sure they were going to good homes where they would be well cared for. I hesitated, because I knew that when my husband lost his beloved spaniel he had sworn never to let another dog into his heart again. But then it occurred to me that this charming little puppy might be just the thing for Mrs Limpley, and I promised my fiend to let her know next day. That evening I put my idea to the Limpleys. Mrs Limpley was silent; she seldom expressed an opinion of her own. However, Limpley himself agreed with his usual enthusiasm. Yes, yes, he said, that was all that had been missing from their lives! A house wasn't really a home without a dog. Impetuous as he was, he tried persuading me to go to Bath with him that very night, rouse my friend and collect the puppy. But when I turned down this fanciful idea he had to wait, and not until the next day did the bulldog puppy arrive at their house in a little basket, yapping and scared by the unexpected journey.

The outcome was not quite what we had expected. I had meant to provide the quiet woman who spent her days alone in an empty house with a companion to share it. However, it was Limpley himself who turned the full force of his inexhaustible need to show affection on the dog. His delight in the comical little creature was boundless, and as always excessive and slightly ridiculous. Of course Ponto, as he called the puppy, I don't know why, was the best-looking, cleverest dog on earth, and Limpley discovered new virtues and talents in him every day, indeed every hour. He spent lavishly on the best equipment for his four-footed friend, on grooming tools, leashes, baskets, a muzzle, food bowls, toys, balls and bones. Limpley studied all the articles and advertisements in the newspapers offering information on the care and nutrition of dogs, and took out a subscription to a dog magazine with a view to acquiring expert knowledge. The large dog industry that makes its money exclusively from such enthusiastic dog-lovers found a new and assiduous customer in him. The least little thing was a reason for a visit to the vet. It would take volumes to describe all the foolish excesses arising in unbroken succession from this new passion of his. We often heard loud barking from the house next door, not from the dog but from his master as he lay flat on the floor, trying to engage his pet in dialogue that no one else could understand by imitating dog language. He paid more attention to the spoilt animal's care than to his own, earnestly following all the dietary advice of dog experts. Ponto ate better than Limpley and his wife, and once, when there was something in the newspaper about typhoid—in a completely different part of the country—the animal was given only bottled mineral water to drink. If a disrespectful flea ventured to come near the sacrosanct puppy and get him scratching or biting in an undignified manner, the agitated Limpley would take the wretched business of flea-hunting upon himself. You would see him in his shirtsleeves, bent over a bucket of water and disinfectant, getting to work with brush and comb until the last unwanted guest had been disposed of. No trouble was too much for him to take, nothing was beneath his dignity, and no prince of the realm could have been more affectionately and carefully looked after than Ponto the puppy. The only good thing to come of all this foolishness was that as a result of Limpley's emotional fixation on his new object of affection, his wife and we were spared a considerable amount of his exuberance; he would spend hours walking the dog and talking to him, although that did not seem to deter the thick-skinned little creature from snuffling around as he liked, and Mrs Limpley watched, smiling and without the slightest jealousy, as her husband carried out a daily ritual at the altar of his four-footed idol. All he withdrew from her in the way off affection was the irritating excess of it, for he still lavished tenderness on her in full measure. We could not help noticing that the new pet in the house had perhaps made their marriage happier than before.

Meanwhile Ponto was growing week by week. The thick puppy folds of his skin filled out with firm, muscular flesh, he grew into a strong animal with a broad chest, strong jaws, and muscular hindquarters that were kept well brushed. He was naturally good-tempered, but he became less pleasant company when he realised that his was the dominant position in the household, and thanks to that he began behaving with lordly arrogance. It had not taken the clever, observant animal long to work out that his master, or rather his slave, would forgive him any kind of naughtiness. First it was just disobedience, but he soon began behaving tyrannically, refusing on principle to do anything that might make him seem subservient. Worst of all, he would allow no one in the house any privacy. Nothing could be done without his presence and, in effect, his express permission. Whenever visitors called he would fling himself imperiously against the door, well knowing that the dutiful Limpley would make haste to open it for him, and then Ponto would jump up proudly into an armchair, not deigning to honour the visitors with so much as a glance. He was showing them that he was the real master of the house, and all honour and veneration were owed to him. Of course no other dog was allowed even to approach the garden fence, and certain people to whom he had taken a dislike, expressed by growling at them, were obliged to put down the post or the milk bottles outside the gate instead of bringing them right up to the house. The more Limpley lowered himself in his childish passion for the now autocratic animal, the worse Ponto treated him, and improbable as it may sound the dog even devised an entire system of ways to show that he might put up with petting and enthusiastic encomiums, but felt not in the least obliged to respond to these daily tributes with any kind of gratitude. As a matter of principle, he kept Limpley waiting every time his master called him, and in the end this unfortunate change in Ponto went so far that he would spend all day racing about as a normal, full-blooded dog who has not been trained in obedience will do, chasing chickens, jumping into the water, greedily devouring anything that came his way, and indulging in his favourite game of racing silently and with malice aforethought down the slope to the canal with the force of a small bomb, head-butting the baskets and tubs of washing standing there until they fell into the water, and then prancing around the washerwomen and girls who had brought them with howls of triumph, while they had to retrieve their laundry from the water item by item. But as soon as it was time for Limpley to come home from the office Ponto, that clever actor, abandoned his high-spirited pranks and assumed the unapproachable air of a sultan. Lounging lazily about, he waited without the slightest welcoming expression for the return of his master, who would fall on him with a hearty, "Hello there, Ponty!" even before he greeted his wife or took off his coat. Ponto did not so much as wag his tail in response. Sometimes he magnanimously rolled over on his back to have his soft, silky stomach scratched, but even at these gracious moments he took care not to show that he was enjoying it by snuffling or grunting with pleasure. His humble servant was to notice that Ponto was doing him a favour by accepting his attentions at all. And with a brief growl that was as much as to say, "That's enough!" he would suddenly turn and put an end to the game. Similarly, he always had to be implored to eat the chopped liver that Limpley fed him piece by piece. Sometimes he merely sniffed at it and despite all persuasions lay down, scorning it, just to show that he was not always to be induced to eat his dinner when his two-legged slave served it up. Invited to go out for a walk, he would begin by stretching lazily, yawning so widely that you could see down to the black spots in his throat. He always insisted on doing something to make it clear that personally he was not

29

much in favour of a walk, and would get off the sofa only to oblige Limpley. All his spoiling made him badly behaved, and he thought up any number of tricks to make sure that his master always assumed the attitude of a beggar and petitioner with him. In fact Limpley's servile passion could well have been described as more like doglike devotion than the conduct of the insubordinate animal, who played the part of oriental pasha to histrionic perfection.

Neither my husband nor I could bear to watch the outrageous behaviour of the tyrannical dog any longer. Clever as he was, Ponto soon noticed our lack of respect for him, and took care to show us his disapproval in the most obvious way. There was no denying that he was a dog of character. After the day when our maid turned him out of the garden in short order when he had left his unmistakable visiting card in one of our rose beds, he never again slipped through the thick hedge that formed the boundary between our two properties, and despite Limpley's pleas and persuasions could not be induced to set foot inside our house. We were glad to dispense with his visits; more awkward was the fact that when we met Limpley in his company walking down the road or outside our house, and that good-natured, talkative man fell into friendly conversation, the tyrannical animal's provocative behaviour made it impossible for us to talk at any length. After two minutes Ponto would begin to howl angrily, or growl and butt Limpley's leg, clearly meaning, "Stop it! Don't talk to these unpleasant people!" And I am sorry to say that Limpley always caved in. First he would try to soothe the disobedient animal. "Just a minute, and then we'll go on." But there was no fobbing off the tyrant, and his unfortunate servant—rather ashamed and confused—would say goodbye to us. Then the haughty animal trotted off, hindquarters proudly raised, visibly triumphant after demonstrating his unlimited power. I am not a violent woman, but my hand always itched to give the spoilt creature a smart blow with a dog whip, just once.

By these means Ponto, a perfectly ordinary dog, had managed to cool our previously friendly relations with our neighbours to a considerable extent. It obviously annoyed Limpley that he could no longer drop in on us every five minutes as he used to; his wife, for her part, was upset because she could see how ridiculous her husband's servile devotion to the dog made him in everyone else's eyes. And so another year passed in little skirmishes of this kind, while the dog became, if possible, even bolder and more demanding, and above all more ingenious in humiliating Limpley, until one day there was a change that surprised all concerned equally. Some of us, indeed, were glad of it, but it was a tragedy for the one most affected.

I had been unable to avoid telling my husband that for the last two or three weeks Mrs Limpley had been curiously shy, avoiding a conversation of any length with me. As good neighbours we lent each other this or that household item from time to time, and these encounters always led to a comfortable chat. I really liked that quiet, modest woman very much. Recently, however, I had noticed that she seemed embarrassed to approach me, and would rather send round her housemaid when she wanted to ask a favour. If I spoke to her, she seemed obviously self-conscious and wouldn't let me look her in the eye. My husband, who had a special liking for her, persuaded me just to go over to her house and ask straight out if we had done something to offend her without knowing it. "One shouldn't let a little coolness of that kind come between neighbours. And maybe it's just the opposite of what you fear. Maybe—and I do think so—she wants to ask you a favour and can't summon up the courage."

I took his advice to heart. I went round to the Limpleys' house and found her sitting in a chair in the garden, so lost in reverie that she didn't even hear me coming. I put a hand on her shoulder and said, speaking frankly, "Mrs Limpley, I'm an old woman and you needn't be shy with me. Let me speak first. If you are annoyed with us about something, do tell me what the matter is."

The poor little woman was startled. How could I think such a thing, she asked? She had kept from visiting me only because … And here she blushed instead of going on, and began to sob, but her sobs were, if I may say so, happy and glad. Finally she told me all about it. After

nine years of marriage she had long ago given up all hope
of being a mother, and even when her suspicion that the
unexpected might have happened had grown stronger in
the last few weeks, she said she hadn't felt brave enough to
believe in it. The day before yesterday, however, she had
secretly gone to see the doctor, and now she was certain.
But she hadn't yet brought herself to tell her husband. I
knew what he was like, she said, she was almost afraid of
his extreme joy. Might it be best—and she hadn't been
able to summon up the courage to ask us—might we be
kind enough to prepare him for the news?

I said we'd be happy to do so. My husband in particular liked the idea, and he set about it with great
amusement. He left a note for Limpley asking him to
come round to us as soon as he got home from the
office. And of course the good man came racing round,
anxious to oblige, without even stopping to take his coat
off. He was obviously afraid that something was wrong
in our house, but on the other hand delighted to let off
steam by showing how friendly and willing to oblige us
he was. He stood there, breathless. My husband asked
him to sit down at the table. This unusual ceremony
alarmed him, and he hardly knew what to do with his
large, heavy, freckled hands.

"Limpley," my husband began, "I thought of you
yesterday evening when I read a maxim in an old book
saying that no one should wish for too much, we should
wish for only a single thing. And I thought to myself—

what would our good neighbour, for instance, wish for if an angel or a good fairy or some other kindly being were to ask him—Limpley, what do you really want in life? I will grant you just one wish."

Limpley looked baffled. He was enjoying the joke, but he did not take it seriously. He still had an uneasy feeling that there was something ominous behind this solemn opening.

"Come along, Limpley, think of me as your good fairy," said my husband reassuringly, seeing him so much at a loss. "Don't you have anything to wish for at all?"

Half-in-earnest, half-laughing, Limpley scratched his short red hair.

"Well, not really," he finally confessed. "I have everything I could want, my house, my wife, my good safe job, my … " I noticed that he was going to say 'my dog', but at the last moment he felt it was out of place. "Yes, I really have all I could wish for."

"So there's nothing for the angel or the fairy to grant you?"

Limpley was getting more cheerful by the minute. He was delighted to be offered the chance to tell us, straight out, how extremely happy he was. "No … not really."

"What a pity," said my husband. "What a pity you can't think of anything." And he fell silent.

Limpley was beginning to feel a little uncomfortable under my husband's searching gaze. He clearly thought he ought to apologise.

"Well, one can always do with a little more money, of course … maybe a promotion at work … but as I said, I'm content … I really don't know what else I could wish for."

"So the poor angel," said my husband, pretending to shake his head sadly, "has to leave his mission unaccomplished because Mr Limpley has nothing to wish for. Well, fortunately the kind angel didn't go straight away again, but had a word with Mrs Limpley first, and he seems to have had better luck with her."

Limpley was taken aback. The poor man looked almost simple-minded, sitting there with his watery eyes staring and his mouth half-open. But he pulled himself together and said with slight irritation, for he didn't see how anyone who belonged to him not be perfectly happy, "My wife? What can *she* have to wish for?"

"Well—perhaps something better than a dog to look after."

Now Limpley understood. He was thunderstruck. Instinctively he opened his eyes so wide in happy surprise that you could see the whites instead of the pupils. All at once he jumped up and ran out, forgetting his coat and without a word of apology to us, storming off to his wife's room like a man demented.

We both laughed. But we were not surprised; it was just what we would have expected of our famously impetuous neighbour.

Someone else, however, *was* surprised. Someone who was lounging on the sofa idly, eyes half-open and blinking, waiting for the homage that his master owed him, or that he thought his master owed him—the well-groomed and autocratic Ponto. But what on earth had happened? The man went rushing past him without a word of greeting or flattery, on into the bedroom, and he heard laughter and weeping and talk and sobs, going on and on, and no one bothered about him, Ponto, who by right and custom received the first loving greeting. An hour passed by. The maid brought him his bowl of food. Ponto scornfully left it untouched. He was used to being begged and urged to eat until he was hand-fed. He growled angrily at the maid. They'd soon find out he wasn't to be fobbed off with indifference like that! But in their excitement his humans never even noticed that he had turned down his dinner that evening. He was forgotten, and forgotten he remained. Limpley was talking on and on to his wife, never stopping, bombarding her with concern and advice, lavishing caresses on her. In the first flush of his delight he had no eyes for Ponto, and the arrogant animal was too proud to remind his master of his existence by intruding. He crouched in a corner and waited. This could only be a misunderstanding, a single if inexcusable oversight. But he waited in vain. Even next morning, when the countless admonitions Limpley kept giving his wife to take it easy and spare herself almost made him miss his bus, he raced out of the house and past Ponto without a word to the dog.

There's no doubt that Ponto was an intelligent animal, but this sudden change was more than he could understand. I happened to be standing at the window when Limpley got on the bus, and I saw how, as soon as he had disappeared inside it, Ponto very slowly—I might almost say thoughtfully—slunk out of the house and watched the vehicle as it drove away. He waited there without moving for half-an-hour, obviously hoping that his master would come back and make up for the attention he had forgotten to pay him the evening before. He did not rush about playing, but only went round and round the house all day slowly, as if deep in thought. Perhaps—who knows how and to what extent sequences of thought can form in an animal mind?—he was brooding on whether he himself had done something clumsy to earn the incomprehensible withdrawal of the favours he was used to. Towards evening, about half-an-hour before Limpley usually came home, he became visibly nervous and kept patrolling the fence with his ears back, keeping an eye open to spot the bus in good time. But of course he wasn't going to show how impatiently he had been waiting; as soon as the bus came into view at its usual hour he hurried back into the living room, lay down on the sofa as usual and waited.

Once again, however, he waited in vain. Once again Limpley hurried past him. And so it went on day after day. Now and then Limpley noticed him, gave him a fleeting, "Oh, there you are, Ponto," and patted him in passing. But it was only an indifferent, casual pat. There was no more flattering, servile attention, there were no more caresses, no games, no walks, nothing, nothing, nothing. Limpley, that fundamentally kindly man, can hardly be blamed for this painful indifference, for he now had no thought in his head but to look after his wife. When he came home from work he accompanied her wherever she went, taking her for walks of just the right length, supporting her with his arm in case she took a hasty or incautious step; he watched over her diet, and made the maid give him a precise report on every hour of her day. Late at night, when she had gone to bed, he came round to our house almost daily to ask me, as a woman of experience, for advice and reassurance; he was already buying equipment in the big department stores for the coming baby. And he did all this in a state of uninterrupted busy excitement. His own personal life came nowhere; sometimes he forgot to shave for two days on end, and sometimes he was late at the office because the constant stream of advice he gave his wife had made him miss the bus. So it was not malice or unfaithfulness if he neglected to take Ponto for walks or pay him attention; only the confusion of a passionate man with an almost monomaniac disposition concentrating all his senses, thoughts and feelings on a single object. But if human beings, in spite of their ability to think logically of the past and the future, are hardly capable of accepting a slight inflicted on them without bearing resentment, how can a dumb animal take it calmly? Ponto was more and more nervous and agitated as the weeks went by. His self-esteem could not tolerate being overlooked and downgraded in importance, when he was the real master of this house. It would have been sensible of him to adopt a pleading, flattering attitude to Limpley, who would then surely have been aware of his dereliction of duty. But Ponto was too proud to crawl to anyone. It was not he but his master who was to make the first approach. So the dog tried all kinds of ruses to draw attention to himself. In the third week he suddenly began limping, dragging his left hind leg as if he had gone lame. In normal circumstances, Limpley would have examined him at once in affectionate alarm, to see if he had a thorn in his paw. He would anxiously have phoned the vet, he would have got up three or four times in the night to see how the dog was doing. Now, however, neither he nor anyone else in the house took the slightest notice of Ponto's pathetically assumed limp, and the embittered dog had no alternative but to put up with it. A couple of weeks later he tried again, this time going on hunger strike. For two days he made the sacrifice of leaving his food untouched. But no one worried about his lack of appetite, whereas usually, if he failed to lick the last morsel out of his bowl in one of his tyrannical moods, the attentive Limpley would fetch him special dog biscuits or a slice of sausage. Finally animal hunger was too much for Ponto, and he secretly and guiltily ate all his food with little enjoyment. Another time he tried to attract attention by hiding for a day. He had prudently taken up quarters in the disused henhouse, where he would be able to listen with satisfaction to anxious cries of "Ponto! Ponto, where are you?" But no one called him, no one noticed his absence or felt worried. His masterful spirit caved in. He had been set aside, humiliated, forgotten, and he didn't even know why.

I think I was the first to notice the change that came over the dog in those weeks. He lost weight, and his bearing was different. Instead of strutting briskly with his hindquarters proudly raised in the old way, he slunk about as if he had been whipped, and his coat, once carefully brushed every day, lost its silky gloss. When you met him he bowed his head so that you couldn't see his eyes and hurried past. But although he had been miserably humiliated, his old pride was not yet entirely broken; he still felt ashamed to face the rest of us, and his only outlet for his fury was to attack those baskets of washing. Within a week he pushed no less than three of them into the canal to make it clear, through his violence, that he was still around and he demanded respect. But even that was no good, and the only effect was that the laundry maids threatened to beat him. All his cunning ruses were in vain—leaving his food, limping, pretending to go missing, assiduously looking for his master—and

he racked his brain inside that square, heavy head—
something mysterious that he didn't understand must
have happened that day. After it, the house and everyone
in it had changed, and the despairing Ponto realised that
he was powerless in the face of whatever had happened
or was still happening. There could be no doubt about
it—someone, some strange and ill-disposed power was
against him. He, Ponto, had an enemy. An enemy who
was stronger than he was, and this enemy was invisible
and out of his reach. So the enemy, that cunning, evil,
cowardly adversary who had taken away all his author-
ity in the household, couldn't be seized, torn to pieces,
bitten until his bones cracked. No sniffing at doorways
helped him, no alert watchfulness, no lying in wait with
ears pricked, no brooding—his enemy, that thief, that
devil, was and remained invisible. In those weeks Ponto
kept pacing along the garden fence like a dog deranged,
trying to find some trace of his diabolical, unseen enemy.

All that his alert senses did pick up was the fact that
preparations of some kind were being made in the house;
he didn't understand them, but they must be to do with
his arch-enemy. Worst of all, there was suddenly an
elderly lady staying there—Mrs Limpley's mother—who
slept at night on the dining-room sofa where Ponto used
to lounge at his ease if his comfortably upholstered basket didn't seem luxurious enough. And then again, all
kinds of things kept being delivered to the house—what
for?—bedclothes, packages, the doorbell was ringing all

the time. Several times a black-clad man with glasses turned up smelling of something horrible, stinking of harsh, inhuman tinctures. The door to the mistress of the house's bedroom was always opening and closing, and there was constant whispering behind it, or sometimes the two ladies would sit together snipping and clicking their sewing things. What did it all mean, and why was he, Ponto, shut out and deprived of his rights? All his brooding finally brought a vacant, almost glazed look to the dog's eyes. What distinguishes an animal's mind from human understanding, after all, is that the animal lives exclusively in the past and the present, and is unable to imagine the future or speculate on what may happen. And here, the dumb animal felt in torments of despair, something was going on that meant him ill, and yet he couldn't defend himself or fight back.

It was six months in all before the proud, masterful, Ponto, exhausted by his futile struggle, humbly capitulated, and oddly enough I was the one to whom he surrendered. I had been sitting in the garden one fine summer evening while my husband played patience indoors, and suddenly I felt the light, hesitant touch of something warm on my knee. It was Ponto, his pride broken. He had not been in our garden for a year-and-a-half, but now, in his distress, he was seeking refuge with me. Perhaps, in those weeks when everyone else was neglecting him, I had spoken to him or patted him in passing, so that he thought of me in this last moment of despair, and I shall never forget the urgent, pleading expression in his eyes as he looked up at me. The glance of an animal in great need can be a more penetrating, I might even say a more speaking look than the glance of a human being, for we put most of our feelings and thoughts into the words with which we communicate, while an animal, incapable of speech, expresses feelings only with its eyes. I have never seen perplexity more touchingly and desperately expressed than I did in that indescribable look from Ponto as he pawed gently at the hem of my skirt, begging. Much moved, I realised that he was saying, "Please tell me what my master and the rest of them have against me. What horrible thing are they planning to do to me in that house? Help me, tell me what to do." I really had no idea what to do myself in view of that pleading look. Instinctively I patted him and murmured under my breath, "Poor Ponto, your time is over. You'll have to get used to it, just as we all have to get used to things we don't like." Ponto pricked up his ears when I spoke to him, and the folds of skin on his brow moved painfully, as if he were trying to guess what my words meant. Then he scraped his paw impatiently on the ground. It was an urgent, restless gesture, meaning something like, "I don't understand you! Explain! Help me!" But I knew there was nothing I could do for him. He must have sensed, deep down, that I had no comfort to offer. He stood up quietly and disappeared as soundlessly as he had come, without looking back.

Ponto was missing for a whole day and a whole night. If he had been human I would have been afraid he had committed suicide. He did not turn up until the evening of the next day, dirty, hungry, scruffy and with a couple of bites; in his helpless fury he must have attacked other dogs somewhere. But new humiliation awaited him. The maid wouldn't let him into the house, but instead put his bowl of food outside the door and then took no more notice of him. It so happened that special circumstances accounted for this cruel insult, because Mrs Limpley had gone into labour, and the house was full of people bustling about. Limpley stood around helplessly, red-faced and trembling with excitement; the midwife was hurrying back and forth, assisted by the doctor; Limpley's mother-in-law was sitting by the bed comforting her daughter; and the maid had her hands more than full. I had come round to the Limpleys' house myself and was waiting in the dining room in case I could be useful in any way. All things considered, Ponto's presence could only have been a nuisance. But how was his dull, doggy brain to understand that? The distressed animal realised only that for the first time he had been turned out of the house—*his* house—like a beggar, unwanted. He was being maliciously kept away from something important going on there behind closed doors. His fury was indescribable, and with his powerful teeth he cracked the bones that had been thrown to him as if they were his unseen enemy's neck. Then he snuffled around; his sharpened senses could tell that other strangers had gone into the house—again, *his* house—and on the drive he picked up the scent of the black-clad man he hated, the man with the glasses. But there were others in league with him as well, and what were they doing in there? The agitated animal listened with his ears pricked up. Pressing close to the wall, he heard voices both soft and loud, groaning, cries, then water splashing, hurried footsteps, things being moved about, the clink of glass and metal—something was going on in there, something he didn't understand. But instinctively he sensed that it was hostile to him. It was to blame for his humiliation, the loss of his rights—it was the invisible, infamous, cowardly, malicious enemy, and now it was really there, now it would be in visible form, now at last he could seize it by the scruff of its neck as it richly deserved. Muscles tense and quivering with excitement, the powerful animal crouched beside the front door so that he could rush in the moment it opened. He wasn't going to get away this time, the evil enemy, the usurper of his rights and privileges who had murdered his peace of mind!

Inside the house no one gave a thought to the dog. We were too busy and excited. I had to reassure and console Limpley—no mean task—when the doctor and the midwife banished him from the bedroom; for those two hours, considering his vast capacity for sympathy, he may well have suffered more than the woman in labour herself. At last came the good news, and after a while Limpley, his feelings vacillating between joy and fear, was cautiously let into the bedroom to see his child—a little girl, as the midwife had just announced—and the new mother. He stayed there for a long time, while his mother-in-law and I, who had been through child-birth ourselves, exchanged reminiscences in friendly conversation.

At last the door opened and Limpley appeared, fol-lowed by the doctor. The proud father was coming to show us the baby, and was carrying her lying on a chang-ing pad, like a priest bearing a monstrance; his broad, kind, slightly simple face almost transfigured by radiant happiness. Tears kept running unstoppably down his cheeks, and he didn't know how to dry them, because his broad hands were holding the child like something inexpressibly precious and fragile. Meanwhile the doc-tor behind him, who was familiar with such scenes, was putting on his coat. "Well, my job here is done," he said smiling, and he shook hands and went to the door, suspecting no harm.

But in the split second when the doctor opened the door, with no idea what was about to happen, something shot past his legs, something that had been crouching there with muscles at full stretch, and there was Ponto in the middle of the room, filling it with the sound of furious barking. He had seen at once that Limpley was holding some new object that he didn't know, holding it tenderly, something small and red and alive that mewed like a cat and smelled human—aha! There was the enemy, the cunning, hidden enemy he had been searching for all this time, the adversary who had robbed him of his power, the creature that had destroyed his peace! Bite it! Tear it to bits! And with bared teeth he leapt up at Limpley to snatch the baby from him. I think we all screamed at the same time, for the powerful animal's movement was so sudden and violent that Limpley, although he was a heavy, sturdily built man, swayed under the weight of the impact and staggered back against the wall. But at the last moment he instinctively held the changing pad up in the air with the baby on it, so that no harm could come to her, and I myself, moving fast, had taken her from Limpley before he fell. The dog immediately turned against me. Luckily the doctor, who had rushed back on hearing our cries, with great presence of mind picked up a heavy chair and flung it. It landed with a heavy impact on the furious animal, cracking bones, as Ponto stood there with his eyes bloodshot and foaming at the mouth. The dog howled with pain and retreated for a moment, only to attack again in his frenzied rage. However, that brief moment had been long enough for Limpley to recover from his fall and fling himself on the dog, in a fury that was horrifyingly like Ponto's own. A terrible battle began. Limpley, a broad, heavy, powerful man, had landed on Ponto with his full weight and was trying to strangle him with his strong hands.

The two of them were now rolling about on the floor in a tangle of limbs as they fought. Ponto snapped, and Limpley went on trying to choke him, his knee braced on the animal's chest, while Ponto kept wriggling out of his grasp. We old women fled into the next room to protect the baby, while the doctor and the maid, joining the fray, now joined the attack on the furious dog. They struck Ponto with anything that came to hand—wood cracked, glass clinked—they went for him with hands and feet, hammering and kicking his body, until the mad barking turned to heavy, stertorous breathing. Finally the animal, now completely exhausted, his breath coming irregularly, had his front and back legs tied by the doctor, the maid and my husband, who had come running from our house when he heard the noise. They used Ponto's own leather leash and some cord, and stuffed a cloth snatched off the table into his mouth. Now entirely defenceless and half-conscious, he was dragged out of the room. Outside the door they got him into a sack, and only then did the doctor hurry back to help.

Limpley, meanwhile, swaying like a drunk, staggered into the other room to make sure his child was all right. The baby was uninjured, and stared up at him with her sleepy little eyes. Nor was his wife in any danger, although she had been woken from her deep, exhausted sleep by all the noise. With some difficulty, she managed to give her husband a wan, affectionate smile as he stroked her hands. Only now was he able to think of

48

himself. He looked terrible, his face white, mad-eyed, his collar torn open and his clothes crumbled and dusty. We were alarmed to see that blood was dripping from his torn right sleeve to the floor. In his fury he had not even noticed that, as he tried to throttle the animal, it had bitten him deeply twice in desperate self-defence. He removed his coat and shirt, and the doctor made haste to bandage his arm. Meanwhile the maid fetched him a brandy, for exhausted by his agitation and the loss of blood he was close to fainting, and it was only with some difficulty that we got him lying down on a sofa. Since he had had little rest for the last two nights as he waited in suspense for the baby's birth, he fell into a deep sleep.

Meanwhile we considered what to do with Ponto. "Shoot him," said my husband, and he was about to go home to fetch his revolver. But the doctor said it was his own duty to take him to have his saliva tested without a moment's delay, in case he was rabid, because if so then special measures must be taken to treat Limpley's bites. He would get Ponto into his car at once, he said. We all went out to help the doctor. The animal was lying defenceless outside the door, bound and gagged—a sight I shall never forget—but he was rolling his bloodshot eyes as if they would pop out of his head. He ground his teeth and retched and swallowed, trying to spit out the gag, while his muscles stood out like cords. His entire contorted body was vibrating and twitching convulsively, and I must confess that although we knew he was well trussed up we all hesitated to touch him. I had never in my life seen anything like such concentrated malice and fury, or such hatred in the eyes of any living creature as in his bloodshot and bloodthirsty gaze. I instinctively wondered if my husband had not been right in suggesting that the dog should be shot at once. But the doctor insisted on taking him away, and so the trussed animal was dragged to his car and driven off, in spite of his helpless resistance.

With this inglorious departure, Ponto vanished from our sight for quite a long time. My husband found out that he had tested negative for rabies under observation for several days at the Pasteur Institute, and as there could be no question of a return to the scene of his crime Ponto had been given to a butcher in Bath who was looking for a strong, aggressive dog. We thought no more of him, and Limpley himself, after wearing his arm in a sling for only two or three days, entirely forgot him. Now that his wife had recovered from the strain of childbirth, his passion and care were concentrated entirely on his little daughter, and I need hardly say that he showed as much extreme and fanatical devotion as to Ponto in his time, and perhaps made even more of a fool of himself. The powerful, heavy man would kneel beside the baby's pram like one of the Magi before the crib in the Nativity scenes of the old Italian masters; every day, every hour, every minute he discovered some new beauty in the little rosy creature, who was indeed a charming child. His quiet, sensible wife smiled with far more understanding on this paternal adoration than on his old senseless idolising of his four-footed friend, and we too benefited, for the presence of perfect, unclouded happiness next door could not help but cast its friendly light on our own house.

We had all, as I said, completely forgotten Ponto when I was surprisingly reminded of him one evening. My husband and I had come back from London late, after going to a concert conducted by Bruno Walter, and I could not drop off to sleep, I don't know why. Was it the echo of the melodies of the Jupiter Symphony that I was unconsciously trying to replay in my head, or was it the mild, clear, moonlit summer night? I got up—it was about two in the morning—and looked out of the window. The moon was sailing in the sky high above, as if drifting before an invisible wind, through clouds that shone silver in its light, and every time it emerged pure and bright from those clouds it bathed the whole garden in snowy brightness. There was no sound; I felt that if a single leaf had stirred it would not have escaped me. So I started in alarm when, in the midst of this absolute silence, I suddenly noticed something moving stealthily along the hedge between our garden and the Limpleys', something black that stood out distinctly as it quietly but restlessly against the moonlit lawn. With instinctive interest, I looked more closely. It was not a

51

living creature, it was nothing corporeal moving there, it was a shadow. Only a shadow, but a shadow that must be cast by some living thing cautiously stealing along under cover of the hedge, the shadow of a human being or an animal. Perhaps I am not expressing myself very well, but the furtive, sly silence of that stealthy shape had something alarming about it. My first thought— for we women worry about such things—was that this must be a burglar, even a murderous one, and my heart was in my mouth. But then the shadow reached the garden hedge on the upper terrace where the fence began, and now it was slinking along past the railing of the fence, curiously hunched. Now I could see the creature itself ahead of its shadow—it was a dog, and I recognised the dog at once. Ponto was back. Very slowly, very cautiously, obviously ready to run away at the first sound, Ponto was snuffling around the Limpleys' house. It was—and I don't know why this thought suddenly flashed through my mind—it was as if he wanted to give notice in advance of something, for his was not the free, loose-limbed movement of a dog picking up a scent; there was something about him suggesting that he had some forbidden or ill-intentioned plan in mind. He did not keep his nose close to the ground, sniffing, nor did he walk with his muscles relaxed, he made his way slowly along, keeping low and almost on his belly, to make himself more inconspicuous. He was inching forward like as if stalking prey. I instinctively leant forward to get a better look at him. But I must have moved clumsily, touching the window frame and making some slight noise, for with a silent leap Ponto disappeared into the darkness. It seemed as if I had only dreamt it all. The garden lay there in the moonlight empty, white and brightly lit again, with nothing moving.

I don't know why, but I felt ashamed to tell my husband about this; it could have been just my senses playing a trick on me. But when I happened to meet the Limpleys' maid in the road next morning, I asked her casually if she had happened to see Ponto again recently. The girl was uneasy, and a little embarrassed, and only when I encouraged her did she admit that yes, she had in fact seen him around several times, and in strange circumstances. She couldn't really say why, but she was afraid of him. Four weeks ago, she told me, she had been taking the baby into town in her pram, and suddenly she had heard terrible barking. As the butcher's van rolled by with Ponto in it, he had howled at her or, as she thought, at the baby in the pram, and looked as if he were crouching to spring, but luckily the van had passed so quickly that he dared not jump out of it. However, she said, his furious barking had gone right through her. Of course she had not told Mr Limpley, she added; the news would only have upset him unnecessarily, and anyway she thought the dog was in safe keeping in Bath. But only the other day, one afternoon when she went out to the old woodshed to fetch a few logs, there had been something moving in there at the back. She had been about to scream in fright, but then she saw it was Ponto hiding there, and he had immediately shot away through the hedge and into our garden. Since then she had suspected that he hid there quite often, and he must have been walking around the house by night, because the other day, after that heavy storm in the night, she had clearly seen paw prints in the wet sand showing that he had circled the whole house several times. Did I think he might want to come back, she asked me? Mr Limpley certainly wouldn't have him in the house again, and living with a butcher Ponto could hardly be hungry. If he were, anyway, he would have come to her in the kitchen first to beg for food. Somehow she didn't like the way he was slinking about the place, she added, and did I think she ought to tell Mr Limpley after all, or at least his wife? We thought it over, and agreed that if Ponto turned up again we would tell his new master the butcher, so that he could put an end to his visits. For the time being, at least, we wouldn't remind Limpley of the existence of the hated animal.

I think we made a mistake, for perhaps—who can say—that might have prevented what happened next day, on that terrible and never-to-be-forgotten Sunday. My husband and I had gone round to the Limpleys', and we were sitting in deckchairs on the small lower terrace of the garden, talking. From the lower terrace, the turf ran down quite a steep slope to the canal. The pram was on the flat lawn of the terrace beside us, and I hardly need say that the besotted father got up in the middle of the conversation every five minutes to enjoy the sight of the baby. After all, she was a pretty child, and on that golden sunlit afternoon it was really charming to see her looking up at the sky with her bright blue eyes and smiling—the hood of the pram was put back—as she tried to pick up the patterns made by the sunlight on her blanket with her delicate if still rather awkward hands. Her father rejoiced at this, as if such miraculous reasoning as hers had never been known, and we ourselves, to give him pleasure, acted as if we had never known anything like it. That sight of her, the last happy moment, is rooted in my mind for ever. Then Mrs Limpley called from the upper terrace, which was in the shade of the veranda, to tell us that tea was ready. Limpley spoke soothingly to the baby as if she could understand him, "There, there, we'll be back in a minute!" We left the pram with the baby in it on the lawn, shaded from the hot sunlight by a cool canopy of leaves above, and strolled slowly to the usual place in the shade where the Limpleys drank afternoon tea. It was about twenty yards from the lower to the upper terrace of their garden, and you could not see one terrace from the other because of the rose-covered pergola between them. We talked as we walked, and I need hardly say what we talked about. Limpley was wonderfully cheerful, but his cheerfulness did not seem at all out of place today, when the sky was such a silky blue, it was such a peaceful Sunday, and we were sitting in the shade in front of a house full of blessings. Today, his mood was like a reflection of that fine summer's day.

Suddenly we were alarmed. Shrill, horrified screams came from the canal, voices of children and women's cries of alarm. We rushed down the green slope with Limpley in the lead. His first thought was for the child. But to our horror the lower terrace, where the pram had been standing only a few minutes ago with the baby dozing peacefully in it in perfect safety, was empty, and the shouting from the canal was shriller and more agitated than ever. We hurried down to the water. On the opposite bank several women and children stood close together, gesticulating and staring at the canal. And there was the pram we had left safe and sound on the lower terrace, now floating upside down in the water. One man had already put out in a boat to save the child, another had dived in. But it was all too late. The baby's body was not brought up from the brackish water, which was covered with green waterweed, until quarter-of-an-hour later.

I cannot describe the despair of the wretched parents. Or rather, I will not even try to describe it, because I never again in my life want to think of those dreadful moments. A police superintendent, informed by telephone, turned up to find out how this terrible thing had happened. Was it negligence on the part of the parents, or an accident, or a crime? The floating pram had been fished out of the water by now, and put back on the lower terrace on the police officer's instructions, just where it had been before. Then the Chief Constable himself joined the superintendent, and personally tested the pram to see whether a light touch would set it rolling down the slope of its own accord. But the wheels would hardly move through the thick, long grass. So it was out of the question for a sudden gust of wind, perhaps, to have made it roll so suddenly over the terrace, which itself was level. The superintendent also tried again, pushing a little harder. The pram rolled about a foot forward and then stopped. But the terrace was at least seven yards wide, and the pram, as the tracks of its wheels showed, had been standing securely some way from the place where the land began to slope. Only when the superintendent took a run up to the pram and pushed it really hard did it move along the terrace and begin to roll down the slope. So something unexpected must have set the pram suddenly in motion. But who or what had done it?

It was a mystery. The police superintendent took his cap off his sweating brow and scratched his short hair ever more thoughtfully. He couldn't make it out. Had any object, he asked, even just a ball when someone was playing with it, ever been known to roll over the terrace and down to the canal of its own accord? "No, never!" everyone assured him. Had there been a child nearby, or in the garden, a high-spirited child who might have been playing with the pram? No, no one! Had there been anyone else in the vicinity? Again, no. The garden gate had been closed, and none of the people walking by the canal had seen anyone coming or going. The one person who could really be regarded as an eyewitness was the labourer who had jumped straight into the water to save the baby, but even he, still dripping wet and greatly distressed, could say only that he and his wife had been walking beside the canal, and nothing seemed wrong. Then the pram had suddenly come rolling down the slope from the garden, going faster and faster, and tipped upside down as soon as it reached the water. As he thought he had seen a child in the water, he had run down to the bank at once, stripping off his jacket, and tried to rescue it, but he had not been able to make his way through the dense tangles of waterweeds as fast as he had hoped. That was all he knew.

The police superintendent was more and more baffled. He had never known such a puzzling case, he said. He simply could not imagine how that pram could have started rolling. The only possibility seemed to be that the baby might suddenly have sat up, or thrown herself violently to one side, thus unbalancing the light-weight pram. But it was hard to believe that, and he for one couldn't imagine it. Was there anything else that occurred to any of us?

I automatically glanced at the Limpleys' housemaid. Our eyes met. We were both thinking the same thing at the same moment. We both knew that the dog hated the child. We knew that he had been seen several times recently slinking around the garden. We knew how he had often head-butted laundry baskets full of washing and sent them into the canal. We both—I saw it from the maid's pallor and her twitching lips—we both suspected that the sly and now vicious animal, finally seeing a chance to get his revenge, had come out of hiding as soon as we left the baby alone for a few minutes, and had then butted the pram containing his hated rival fiercely and fast, sending it rolling down to the canal, before making his own escape as soundlessly as usual. But we neither of us voiced our suspicions. I knew the mere idea that if he had shot the raving animal after Ponto's attack, he might have saved his child would drive Limpley mad. And then, in spite of the logic of our thinking, we lacked any solid evidence. Neither the maid nor I, and none of the others, had actually seen the dog slinking around or running away that afternoon. The woodshed where he liked to hide—I looked there at once—was empty, the dry trodden earth of its floor showed no trace at all, we had not heard a note of the furious barking in which Ponto had always triumphantly indulged when he pushed a basket of washing into the canal. So we could not really claim that he had done it. It was more of a cruelly tormenting assumption. Only a justified, a terribly well justified suspicion. But the final, clinching certainty was missing.

And yet I have never since shaken off that dreadful suspicion—on the contrary, it was even more strongly confirmed over the next few days, almost to the point of certainty. A week later—the poor baby had been buried by then, and the Limpleys had left the house because they could not bear the sight of that fateful canal—something happened that affected me deeply. I had been shopping in Bath for a few household items when I suddenly had a shock. Beside the butcher's van I saw Ponto, of whom I had subconsciously been thinking in all those terrible hours, walking along at his leisure, and at the same moment he saw me. He stopped at once, and so did I. And now something that still weighs on my mind happened; in all the weeks that had passed since his humiliation, I had never seen Ponto looking anything but upset and distressed, and he had avoided any encounter with me, crouching low and turning his eyes away. Now he held his head high and looked at me—I can't put it any other way—with self-confident indifference. Overnight he had become the proud, arrogant animal of the old days again. He stood in that provocative position for a minute. Then, swaggering and almost dancing across the road with pretended friendliness, he came over to me and stopped a foot or so away, as if to say, "Well, here I am! Now what have you got to say? Are you going to accuse me?"

I felt paralysed. I had no power to push him away, no power to bear that self-confident and, indeed, I might almost say self-satisfied look. I walked quickly on. God forbid I should accuse even an innocent animal, let alone a human being, of a crime he did not commit. But since that day I cannot get rid of the terrible thought: "He did it. He was the one who did it."

THE MIRACLES
OF LIFE

To my dear friend Hans Müller

G REY MIST LAY LOW over Antwerp, enveloping the city entirely in its dense and heavy swathes. The shapes of houses were blurred in the fine, smoky vapour, and you could not see to the end of the street, but overhead there was ringing in the air, a deep sound like the word of God coming out of the clouds, for the muted voices of the bells in the church towers, calling their congregations to prayer, had also merged in the great, wild sea of mist filling the city and the countryside around, and encompassing the restless, softly roaring waters of the sea far away in the harbour. Here and there a faint gleam struggled against the damp grey mist, trying to light up a gaudy shop sign, but only muffled noise and throaty laughter told you where to find the taverns in which freezing customers gathered, complaining of the weather. The alleys seemed empty, and any passers-by were seen only as fleeting impressions that soon dissolved into the mist. It was a dismal, depressing Sunday morning.

Only the bells called and pealed as if desperately, while the mist stifled their cries. For the devout were few and far between; foreign heresy had found a foothold in this land, and even those who had not abandoned their old faith were less assiduous and zealous in the service of the Lord. Heavy morning mists were enough to keep many away from their devotions. Wrinkled old women busily telling their beads, poor folk in their plain Sunday best stood looking lost in the long, dark aisles of the churches, where the shining gold of altars and chapels and the priests' bright chasubles shone like a mild and gentle flame. But the mist seemed to have seeped through the high walls, for here, too, the chilly and sad mood of the deserted streets prevailed. The morning sermon itself was cold and austere, without a ray of sunlight to brighten it. It was preached against the Protestants, and the driving force behind it was furious rage, hatred along with a strong sense of power, for the time for moderation was over, and good news from Spain had reached the clerics—the new king served the work of the Church with admirable fervour. In his sermon, the preacher united graphic descriptions of the Last Judgement with dark words of admonition for the immediate future. If there had been a large congregation, his words might have been passed on by the faithful murmuring in their pews to a great crowd of hearers, but as it was they dropped into the dark void with a dull echo, as if frozen in the moist, chilly air.

During the storm two men had quickly entered the main porch of the cathedral, their faces obscured at first by wind-blown hair and voluminous coats with collars turned up high. The taller man shed his damp coat to reveal the honest but not especially striking features of a portly man in the rich clothing suitable for a merchant. The other was a stranger figure, although not because of anything unusual in his clothing; his gentle, unhurried movements and his rather big-boned, rustic but kindly face, surrounded by abundant waving white hair, lent him the mild aspect of an evangelist. They both said a short prayer, and then the merchant signed to his older companion to follow him. They went slowly, with measured steps, into the side aisle, which was almost entirely in darkness because dank air made the candles gutter, and heavy clouds that refused to lift still obscured the bright face of the sun. The merchant stopped at one of the small side chapels, most of which contained devotional items promised to the Church as donations by the old families of the city, and pointing to one of the little altars he said, "Here it is."

The other man came closer and shaded his eyes with his hand to see it better in the dim light. One wing of the altarpiece was occupied by a painting in clear colours made even softer by the twilight, and it immediately caught the old painter's eye. It showed the Virgin Mary, her heart transfixed by a sword, and despite the pain and sorrow of the subject it was a gentle work with an aura of reconciliation about it. Mary had a strangely sweet face, not so much that of the Mother of God as of a dreaming girl in the bloom of youth, but with the idea of pain tingeing the smiling beauty of a playful, carefree nature. Thick black hair tumbling down softly surrounded a small, pale but radiant face with very red lips, glowing like a crimson wound. The features were wonderfully delicate, and many of the brushstrokes, for instance in the assured, slender curve of the eyebrows, gave an almost yearning expression to the beauty of the tender face. The Virgin's dark eyes were deep in thought, as if dreaming of another brighter and sweeter world from which her pain was stealing her away. The hands were folded in gentle devotion, and her breast still seemed to be quivering with slight fear at the cold touch of the sword piercing her. Blood from her wound ran along it. All this was bathed in a wonderful radiance surrounding her head with golden flame, and even her heart glowed like the mystical light of the chalice in the stained glass of the church windows when sunlight fell through them. And the twilight around it took the last touch of worldliness from this picture, so that the halo around the sweet girlish face shone with the true radiance of transfiguration.

Almost abruptly, the painter tore himself away from his lengthy admiration of the picture. "None of our countrymen painted this," he said

The merchant nodded in agreement.

"No, it is by an Italian. A young painter at the time. But there's quite a long story behind it. I will tell it all to you from the beginning, and then, as you know, I want you to complete the altarpiece by putting the keystone in place. Look, the sermon is over. We should find a better place to tell stories than this church, well as it may suit our joint efforts. Let's go."

The painter lingered for a moment longer before turning his eyes away from the picture. It seemed even more radiant as the smoky darkness outside the windows lifted, and the mist took on a golden hue. He almost felt that if he stayed here, rapt in devout contemplation of the gentle pain on those childish lips, they would smile and reveal new loveliness. But his companion had gone ahead of him already, and he had to quicken his pace to catch up with the merchant in the porch. They left the cathedral together, as they had come.

The heavy cloak of mist thrown over the city by the early spring morning had given way to a dull, silvery light caught like a cobweb among the gabled roofs. The close-set cobblestones had a steely, damp gleam, and the first of the flickering sunlight was beginning to cast its gold on them. The two men made their way down narrow, winding alleys to the clear air of the harbour, where the merchant lived. And as they slowly walked towards it at their leisure, deep in thought and lost in memory, the merchant's story gathered pace.

"As I have told you already," he began, "I spent some time in Venice in my youth. And to cut a long story short, my conduct there was not very Christian. Instead of managing my father's business in the city, I sat in taverns with young men who spent all day carousing and making merry, drinking, gambling, often bawling out some bawdy song or uttering bitter curses, and I was just as bad as the others. I had no intention of going home. I took life easy and ignored my father's letters when he wrote to me more and more urgently and sternly, warning me that people in Venice who knew me had told him that my licentious life would be the end of me. I only laughed, sometimes with annoyance, and a quick draught of sweet, dark wine washed all my bitterness away, or if not that then the kiss of a wanton girl. I tore up my father's letters, I had abandoned myself entirely to a life of intoxicated frenzy, and I did not intend to give it up. But one evening I was suddenly free of it all. It was very strange, and sometimes I still feel as if a miracle had cleared my path. I was sitting in my usual tavern; I can still see it today, with its smoke and vapours and my drinking companions. There were girls of easy virtue there as well, one of them very beautiful, and we seldom made merrier than that night, a stormy and very strange one. Suddenly, just as a lewd story aroused roars of laughter, my servant came in with a letter for me brought by the courier from Flanders. I was displeased. I did not like receiving my father's letters, which were always admonishing me to do my duty and be a good Christian, two notions that I had long ago drowned in wine. But I was about to take it from the servant when up jumped one of my drinking companions, a handsome, clever fellow, a master of all the arts of chivalry. 'Never mind the croaking old toad. What's it to you?' he cried, throwing the letter up in the air, swiftly drawing his sword, neatly spearing the letter as it fluttered down and pinning it to the wall. The supple blue blade quivered as it stuck there. He carefully withdrew the sword, and the letter, still unopened, stayed where it was. 'There clings the black bat!' he laughed. The others applauded, the girls clustered happily around him, they drank his health. I laughed myself, drank with them, and forgetting the letter and my father, God and myself, I forced myself into wild merriment. I gave the letter not a thought, and we went on to another tavern, where our merriment turned to outright folly. I was drunk as never before, and one of those girls was as beautiful as sin."

The merchant instinctively stopped and passed his hand several times over his brow, as if to banish an unwelcome image from his mind. The painter was quick to realise that this was a painful memory, and did not look at him, but let his eyes rest with apparent interest on a galleon under full sail, swiftly approaching the harbour that the two men had reached, and where they now stood amidst all its colourful hurry and bustle. The merchant's silence did not last long, and he soon continued his tale.

"You can guess how it was. I was young and bewildered, she was beautiful and bold. We came together, and I was full of urgent desire. But a strange thing happened. As I lay in her amorous embrace, with her mouth pressed to mine, I did not feel the kiss as a wild gesture of affection willingly returned. Instead, I was miraculously

71

reminded of the gentle evening kisses we exchanged in my parental home. All at once, strange to say, even as I lay in the whore's arms I thought of my father's crumpled, mistreated, unread letter, and it was as if I felt my drinking companion's sword-thrust in my own bleeding breast. I sat up, so suddenly and looking so pale that the girl asked in alarm what the matter was. However, I was ashamed of my foolish fears, ashamed in front of this woman, a stranger, in whose bed I lay and whose beauty I had been enjoying. I did not want to tell her the foolish thoughts of that moment. Yet my life changed there and then, and today I still feel, as I felt at the time, that only the grace of God can bring such a change. I threw the girl some money, which she took reluctantly because she was afraid I despised her, and she called me a German fool. But I listened to no more from her, and instead stormed away on that cold, rainy night, calling like a desperate man over the dark canals for a gondola. At last one came along, and the price the gondolier asked was high, but my heart was beating with such sudden, merciless, incomprehensible fear that I could think of nothing but the letter, miraculously reminded of it as I suddenly was. By the time I reached the tavern my desire to read it was like a devouring fever; I raced into the place like a madman, ignoring the cheerful, surprised cries of my companions, jumped up on a table, making the glasses on it clink, tore the letter down from the wall and ran out again, taking no notice of the derision and angry curses behind me. At the first corner I unfolded the letter with trembling hands. Rain was pouring down from the overcast sky, and the wind tore at the sheet of paper in my hands. However, I did not stop reading until, with overflowing eyes, I had deciphered the whole of the letter. Not that the words in it were many—they told me that my mother was sick and likely to die, and asked me to come home. Not a word of the usual blame or reproach. But how my heart burnt with shame when I saw that the sword blade had pierced my mother's name ... "

"A miracle indeed, an obvious miracle, one to be understood not by everyone but certainly by the man affected," murmured the painter as the merchant, deeply moved, lapsed into silence. For a while they walked along side by side without a word. The merchant's fine house was already visible in the distance, and when he looked up and saw it he quickly went on with his tale.

"I will be brief. I will not tell you what pain and remorseful madness I felt that night. I will say only that next morning found me kneeling on the steps of St Mark's in ardent prayer, vowing to donate an altar to the Mother of God if she would grant me the grace to see my mother again alive and receive her forgiveness. I set off that same day, travelling for many days and hours in despair and fear to Antwerp, where I hurried in wild desperation to my parental home. At the gate stood my mother herself, looking pale and older, but restored to good health. On seeing me she opened her arms to me, rejoicing, and in her embrace I wept tears of sorrow pent up over many days and many shamefully wasted nights. My life was different after that, and I may almost say it was a life well lived. I have buried that letter, the dearest thing I had, under the foundation stone of this house, built by the fruits of my own labour, and I did my best to keep my vow. Soon after my return here I had the altar that you have seen erected, and adorned as well as I could. However, as I knew nothing of those mysteries by which you painters judge your art, and wanted to dedicate a worthy picture to the Mother of God, who had worked a miracle for me, I wrote to a good friend in Venice asking him to send me the best of the painters he knew, to paint me the work that my heart desired.

"Months passed by. One day a young man came to my door, told me what his calling was, and brought me greetings and a letter from my friend. This Italian painter, whose remarkable and strangely sad face I well remember to this day, was not at all like the boastful, noisy drinking companions of my days in Venice. You might have thought him a monk rather than a painter, for he wore a long, black robe, his hair was cut in a plain style, and his face showed the spiritual pallor of asceticism and night watches. The letter merely confirmed my favourable impression, and dispelled any doubts aroused in me by the youthfulness of this Italian master. The older painters of Italy, wrote my friend, were prouder than princes, and even the most tempting offer could not lure them away from their native land, where they were surrounded by great lords and ladies as well as the common people. He had chosen this young master because, for some reason he did not know, the young man's wish to leave Italy weighed more with him than any offer of money, but the young painter's talent was valued highly and honoured in his own country.

"The man my friend had sent was quiet and reserved. I never learnt anything about his life beyond hints that a beautiful woman had played a painful part in his story, and it was because of her that he had left his native Italy. And although I have no proof of it, and such an idea seems heretical and unchristian, I think that the picture you have seen, which he painted within a few weeks without a model, working with careful preparation from memory, bears the features of the woman he had loved. Whenever I came to see him at work I found him painting another version of that same sweet face again, or lost in dreamy contemplation of it. Once the painting was finished, I felt secretly afraid of the godlessness of painting a woman who might be a courtesan as the Mother of God, and asked him to choose a different model for the companion piece that I also wanted. He did not reply, and when I went to see him next day he had left without a word of goodbye. I had some scruples about adorning the altar with that picture, but the priest whom I consulted felt no such doubt in accepting it."

"And he was right," interrupted the painter, almost vehemently. "For how can we imagine the beauty of Our Lady if not from looking at the woman we see in the picture? Are we not made in God's image? If so such a portrayal, if only a faint copy of the unseen original must be the closest to perfection that we can offer to human eyes. Now, listen—you want me to paint that second picture. I am one of those poor souls who cannot paint without a living model. I do not have the gift of painting only from within myself, I work from nature in trying to show what is true in it. I would not choose a woman whom I myself loved to model for a portrait worthy of the Mother of God—it would be sinful to see the immaculate Virgin through her face—but I would look for a lovely model and paint the woman whose features seem to me to show the face of the Mother of God as I have seen it in devout dreams. And believe me, although those may be the features of a sinful human woman, if the work is done in pious devotion none of the dross of desire and sin will be left. The magic of such purity, like a miraculous sign, can often be expressed in a woman's face. I think I have often seen that miracle myself."

"Well, however that may be, I trust you. You are a mature man, you have endured and experienced much, and if you see no sin in it … "

"Far from it! I consider it laudable. Only Protestants and other sectarians denounce the adornment of God's house."

"You are right. But I would like you to begin the picture soon, because my vow, still only half-fulfilled, still burns in me like a sin. For twenty years I forgot about the second picture in the altarpiece. Then, quite recently, when I saw my wife's sorrowful face as she wept by our child's sickbed, I thought of the debt I owed and renewed my vow. And as you are aware, once again the Mother of God worked a miracle of healing, when all the doctors had given up in despair. I beg you not to leave it too long before you start work."

"I will do what I can, but to be honest with you, never in my long career as an artist has anything struck me as so difficult. If my picture is not to look a poor daub, carelessly constructed, beside the painting of that young master—and I long to know more about his work—then I shall need to have the hand of God with me."

"God never fails those who are loyal to him. Goodbye, then, and go cheerfully to work. I hope you will soon bring good news to my house."

The merchant shook hands cordially with the painter once again outside the door of his house, looking confidently into the artist's clear eyes, set in his honest German, angular face like the waters of a bright mountain lake surrounded by weathered peaks and rough rocks. The painter had another parting remark on his lips, but left it unspoken and firmly clasped the hand offered to him. The two parted in perfect accord with each other.

The painter walked slowly along beside the harbour, as he always liked to do when his art did not keep him to his studio. He loved the busy, colourful scene presented by the place, with the hurry and bustle of work at the waterside, and sometimes he sat down on a bollard to sketch the curious physical posture of a labourer, or practice the difficult knack of foreshortening a path only a foot wide. He was not at all disturbed by the loud cries of the seamen, the rattling of carts and the monotonous sound of the sea breaking on shore. He had been granted those insights that do not reflect images seen only in the mind's eye, but can recognise in every living thing, however humble or indifferent, the ray of light to illuminate a work of art. For that reason he always liked places where life was at its most colourful, offering a confusing abundance of different delights. He walked among the sailors slowly, with a questing eye, and no one dared to laugh at him, for among all the noisy, useless folk who gather in a harbour, just as the beach is covered with empty shells and pebbles, he stood out with his calm bearing and the dignity of his appearance.

This time, however, he soon gave up his search and got to his feet. The merchant's story had moved him deeply. It touched lightly upon an incident in his own life, and even his usual devotion to the magic of art failed him today. The mild radiance of that picture of the Virgin painted by the young Italian master seemed to illuminate the faces of all the women he saw today, even if they were only stout fishwives. Dreaming and thoughtful, he wandered indecisively for a while past the crowd in its Sunday best, but then he stopped trying to resist his longing to go back to the cathedral and look at the strange portrayal of that beautiful woman again.

A few weeks had passed since the conversation in which the painter agreed to his friend's request for a second picture to complete the altarpiece for the Mother of God, and still the blank canvas in his studio looked reproachfully at the old master. He almost began to fear it, and spent a good deal of time out and about in the streets of the city to keep himself from brooding on its stern admonition and his own despondency. In a life full of busy work—perhaps he had in fact worked *too* hard, failing to keep an enquiring eye on his true self—a change had come over the painter since he first set eyes on the young Italian's picture. Future and past had been wrenched abruptly apart, and looked at him like an empty mirror reflecting only darkness and shadows. And nothing is more terrible than to feel that your life's final peak of achievement already lies just ahead if only you stride on boldly, and then be assailed by a brooding fear that you have taken the wrong path, you have lost your power, you cannot take the last, least step forward. All at once the artist, who had painted hundreds of sacred pictures in the course of his life, seemed to have lost his ability to portray a human face well enough for him to think it worthy of a divine subject. He had looked at women who sold their faces as artist's models to be copied by the hour, at others who sold their bodies, at citizens' wives and gentle girls with the light of inner purity shining in their faces, but whenever they were close to him, and he was on the point of painting the first brushstroke on the canvas, he was aware of their humanity. He saw the blonde, greedy plump figure of one, he saw another's wild addiction to the game of love; he sensed the smooth emptiness behind the brief gleam of a girlish brow, and was disconcerted by the bold gait of whores and the immodest way they swung their hips. Suddenly a world full of such people seemed a bleak place. He felt that the breath of the divine had been extinguished, quenched by the exuberant flesh of these desirable women who knew nothing about mystical virginity, or the tremor of awe in immaculate devotion to dreams of another world. He was ashamed to open the portfolios containing his own work, for it seemed to him as if he had, so to speak, made himself unworthy to live on this earth, had committed a sin in painting pictures where sturdy country folk modelled for the Saviour's disciples and stout countrywomen as the women who served him. His mood became more and more sombre and oppressive. He remembered himself as a young man following his father's plough, long before he took to art instead, he saw his hard peasant hands thrusting the harrow through the black earth, and wondered if he would not have done better to sow yellow seed corn and work to support a family, instead of touching secrets and miraculous signs, mysteries not meant for him, with his clumsy fingers. His whole life seemed to be turned upside down, he had run aground on the fleeting vision of an hour when he saw an image that came back to him in his dreams, and was both torment and blessing in his waking moments. For he could no longer see the Mother of God in his prayers except as she was in the picture that presented so lovely a portrayal of her. It was so different from the beauty of all the earthly women he met, transfigured in the light of feminine humility touched with a presentiment of the divine. In the deceptive twilight of memory, the images of all the women he had ever loved came together in that wonderful figure. And when he tried, for the first time, to ignore reality and create a Mother of God out of the figure of Mary with her child that hovered before his mind's eye, smiling gently in happy, unclouded bliss, then his fingers, wielding the brush, sank powerless as if numbed by cramp. The current was drying up, the skill of his fingers in interpreting the words spoken by the eye seemed helpless in the face of his bright dream, although he saw as clearly in his imagination as if it were painted on a solid wall. His inability to give shape to the fairest and truest of his dreams and bring it into reality was pain that burnt like fire now that reality itself, in all

81

its abundance, did not help him to build a bridge. And he asked himself a terrible question—could he still call himself an artist if such a thing could happen to him, had he been only a hardworking craftsman all his life, fitting colours together as a labourer constructs a building out of stones?

Such self-tormenting reflections gave him not a day's rest, and drove him with compelling power out of his studio, where the empty canvas and carefully prepared tools of his trade reproached him like mocking voices. Several times he thought of confessing his dilemma to the merchant, but he was afraid that the latter, while a pious and well-disposed man, would never understand him, and would think it more of a clumsy excuse than real inability to begin such a work. After all, he had already painted many sacred pictures, to the general acclaim of laymen and master painters alike. So he made it his habit to wander the streets, restless and at his wits' end, secretly alarmed when chance or a hidden magic made him wake from his wandering dreams again and again, finding himself outside the cathedral with the altarpiece in its chapel, as if there were an invisible link between him and the picture, or a divine power ruled his soul even in dreams. Sometimes he went in, half-hoping to find some flaw in the picture and thus break free of its spell, but in front of it he entirely forgot to assess the young artist's creation enviously, judging its art and skill. Instead, he felt the rushing of wings around him, bearing him up into spheres of calm, transfigured contemplation. It was not until he left the cathedral and began thinking of himself and his own efforts that he felt the old pain again, redoubled.

One afternoon he had been wandering through the colourful streets once more, and this time he felt that his tormenting doubt was eased. The first breath of spring wind had begun to blow from the south, bringing with it the brightness, if not the warmth, of many fine spring days to come. For the first time the dull grey gloom that his own cares had cast over the world seemed to leave the painter, and a sense of the grace of God poured into his heart, as it always did when fleeting signs of spring announced the great miracle of resurrection. A clear March sun washed all the rooftops and streets clean, brightly coloured pennants fluttered down in the harbour, the water shone blue between the ships rocking gently there, and the never-ending noise of the city was like jubilant song. A troop of Spanish cavalry trotted over the main square. No hostile glances were cast at them today; the townsfolk enjoyed the sight of the sun reflected from their armour and shining helmets. Women's white headdresses, tugged wilfully back by the wind, revealed fresh, highly coloured complexions. Wooden clogs clattered on the cobblestones as children danced in a ring, holding hands and singing.

And in the usually dark alleys of the harbour district, to which the artist now turned feeling ever lighter at heart, something shimmering flickered like a falling rain of light. The sun could not quite show its bright face between the gabled roofs here as they leant towards each other, densely crowded together, black and crumpled like the hoods of a couple of little old women standing there chattering, one each side of the street. But the light was reflected from window to window, as if sparkling hands were waving in the air, passing back and forth in a high-spirited game. In many places the light remained soft and muted, like a dreaming eye in the first evening twilight. Down below in the street lay darkness where it had lain for years, hidden only occasionally in winter by a cloak of snow. Those who lived there had the sad gloom of constant dusk in their eyes, but the children who longed for light and brightness trusted the enticement of these first rays of spring, playing in their thin clothing on the dirty, potholed streets. The narrow strip of blue sky showing between the rooftops, the golden dance of the sunlight above made them deeply, instinctively happy.

The painter walked on and on, never tiring. He felt as if he, too, were granted secret reasons to rejoice, as if every spark of sunlight was the fleeting reflection of the radiance of God's grace going to his heart. All the bitterness had left his face. It now shone with such a mild and kindly light that the children playing their games were amazed, and greeted him with awe, thinking that he must be a priest. He walked on and on, with never a thought for where he was going. The new force of springtime was in his limbs, just as flower buds tap hopefully at the bast holding old, weather-beaten trees together, willing it to let their young strength shoot out into the light. His step was as spry and light as a young man's, and he seemed to be feeling fresher and livelier even though he had been walking for hours, putting stretches of the road behind him at a faster and more flexible pace.

Suddenly the painter stopped as if turned to stone and shaded his eyes with his hand to protect them, like a man dazzled by a flashing light or some awesome, incredible event. Looking up at a window, he had felt the full beam of sunlight reflected back from it strike his eyes painfully, but through the crimson and gold mist forming in front of them a strange apparition, a wonderful illusion had appeared—there was the Madonna painted by that young Italian master, leaning back dreamily and with a touch of sorrow as she did in the picture. A shudder ran through him as the terrible fear of disappointment united with the trembling ecstasy of a man granted grace, one who had seen a vision of the Mother of God not in the darkness of a dream but in bright daylight. That was a miracle of the kind to which many had borne witness, but few had really seen it! He dared not look up yet, his trembling shoulders did not feel strong enough to bear the shattering effect of finding that he was wrong, and he was afraid that this one moment could crush his life even more cruelly than the merciless self-torment of his despairing heart. Only when his pulse was beating more steadily and slowly, and he no longer felt it like a hammer blow in his throat, did he pull himself together and look up slowly from the shelter of his hand at the window where he had seen that seductive image framed.

He had been mistaken. It was not the girl from the young master's Madonna. Yet all the same, his raised hand did not sink despondently. What he saw also appeared to him a miracle, if a sweeter, milder, more human one than a divine apparition seen in the radiant light of a blessed hour. This girl, looking thoughtfully out of the sunlit window frame, bore only a distant resemblance to the altarpiece in the chapel—her face too was framed by black hair, she too had a delicate complexion of mysterious, fantastic pallor, but her features were harder, sharper, almost angry, and around the mouth there was a tearful defiance that was not moderated even by the lost expression of her dreaming eyes, which held an old, deep grief. There was a childlike wilfulness and a legacy of hidden sorrow in their bright restlessness, which she seemed to control only with difficulty. He felt that her silent composure could dissolve into abrupt and angry movement at any time, and her mood of gentle reverie did not hide it. The painter felt a certain tension in her features, suggesting that this child would grow to be one of those women who live in their dreams and are at one with their longings, whose souls cling to what they love with every fibre of their being, and who die if they are forced away from it. But he marvelled not so much at all this strangeness in her face as at the miraculous play of nature that made the sunny glow behind her head, reflected in the window, look like a saint's halo lying around her hair until it shone like black steel. And he thought he clearly felt here the divine hand showing him how to complete his work in a manner worthy of the subject and pleasing to God.

A carter roughly jostled the painter as he stood in the middle of the street, lost in thought. "God's wrath, can't you watch out, old man, or are you so taken with the lovely Jew girl that you stand there gaping like an idiot and blocking my way?"

The painter started with surprise, but took no offence at the man's rough tone, and indeed he had scarcely noticed it in the light of the information provided by this gruff and heavily clad fellow. "Is she Jewish?" he asked in great surprise.

"So it's said, but I don't know. Anyway, she's not the child of the folk here, they found her or came by her somehow. What's it to me? I've never felt curious about it, and I won't neither. Ask the master of the house himself if you like. He'll know better than me, for sure, how she comes to be here."

The 'master' to whom he referred was an innkeeper, landlord of one of those dark, smoky taverns where the liveliness and noise never quite died down, because it was frequented by so many gamblers and seamen, soldiers and idlers that the place was seldom left entirely empty. Broad-built, with a fleshy but kindly face, he stood in the narrow doorway like an inn sign inviting custom. On impulse the painter approached him. They went into the tavern, and the painter sat down in a corner at a smeared wooden table. He still felt rather agitated, and when the landlord put the glass he had ordered in front of him, he asked him to sit at the table with him for a few moments. Quietly, so as not to attract the attention of a couple of slightly tipsy sailors bawling out songs at the next table, he asked his question. He told the man briefly but with deep feeling of the miraculous sign that had appeared to him—the landlord listened in surprise as his slow understanding, somewhat clouded by wine, tried to follow the painter—and finally asked if he would allow him to paint his daughter as the model for a picture of the Virgin Mary. He did not forget to mention that by giving permission her father too would be taking part in a devout work, and pointed out several times that he would be ready to pay the girl good money for her services.

The innkeeper did not answer at once, but kept rubbing his broad nostrils with a fat finger. At last he began.

"Well, sir, you mustn't take me for a bad Christian, by God no, but it's not as easy as you think. If I was her father and I could say to my daughter, off you go and do as I say, well, sir, the bargain would soon be struck.

But with that child, it's different … Good God, what's the matter?"

He had jumped up angrily, for he did not like to be disturbed as he talked. At another table a man was hammering his empty tankard on the bench and demanding another. Roughly, the landlord snatched the tankard from his hand and refilled it, suppressing a curse. At the same time he picked up a glass and bottle, went back to join his new guest, sat down and filled glasses for them both. His own was soon gulped down, and as if well refreshed he wiped his bristling moustache and began his tale.

"I'll tell you how I came by that Jewish girl, sir. I was a soldier, fighting first in Italy, then in Germany. A bad trade, I can tell you, never worse than today, and it was bad enough even back then. I'd had enough of it, I was on my way home through Germany to take up some honest calling, because I didn't have much left to call my own. The money you get as loot in warfare runs through your fingers like water, and I was never a skinflint. So I was in some German town or other, I'd only just arrived, when I heard a great to-do that evening. What set it off I don't know, but the townsfolk had ganged up together to attack the local Jews and I went along with them, partly hoping to pick something up, partly out of curiosity to see what happened. The townsfolk went to work with a will, there was storming of houses, killing, robbing, raping, and the men of the town were roaring with greed and lust. I'd soon had enough of that kind of thing, and I left them to it. I wasn't going to sully my honourable sword with women's blood, or wrestle with whores for what loot I could find. Well then, as I'm about to go back down a side alley, I see an old Jew with his long beard a-quiver, his face distorted, holding in his arms a small child just woken from sleep. He runs to me and stammers out a torrent of words I can't make out. All I understood of his Yiddish German was that he'd give me a good sum of money in return for saving the pair of them. I felt sorry for the child, looking at me all alarmed with her big eyes. And it didn't seem a bad bargain, so I threw my cloak over the old man and took them to my lodgings. There was a few people standing in the alleys, looking like they were inclined to go for the old man, but I'd drawn my sword, and they let all three of us pass. I took them to the inn where I was staying, and when the old man went on his knees to plead with me we left the town that same evening, while the fire-raising and murder went on into the night. We could still see the firelight when we were far away, and the old man stared at it in despair, but the child, she just slept on calmly. The three of us weren't together for long. After a few days the old man fell mortally sick, and he died on the way. But first he gave me all the money he'd brought away with him, and a piece of paper written in strange letters—I was to give a broker in Antwerp, he said, and he told me the man's name. He commended his granddaughter to my care as he died. Well, I came here to Antwerp and showed that piece of paper, and a strange effect it had too—the broker gave me a handsome sum of money, more than I'd have expected. I was glad of it, for now I could be free of the wandering life, so I bought this house and the tavern with the money and soon forgot the war. I kept the child. I was sorry for her, and then I hoped that as she grew up she'd do the work about the place for me, old bachelor that I am. But it didn't turn out like that.

"You saw her just now, and that's the way she is all day. She looks out of the window at empty air, she speaks to no one, she gives timid answers as if she was ducking down expecting someone to hit her. She never speaks to men. At first I thought she'd be an asset here in the tavern, bringing in the guests, like the landlord's young daughter over the road, she'll joke with his customers and encourage them to drink glass after glass. But our girl here's not bold, and if anyone so much as touches her she screams and runs out of the door like a whirlwind. And then if I go looking for her she's sure to be sitting huddled in a corner somewhere, crying fit to break your heart, you'd think God know what harm had come to her. Strange folk, the Jews!"

"Tell me," said the painter, interrupting the storyteller, who was getting more and more thoughtful as he went on, "tell me, is she still of the Jewish religion, or has she converted to the true faith?"

The landlord scratched his head in embarrassment. "Well, sir," he said, "I was a soldier. I couldn't say too much about my own Christianity. I seldom went to church and I don't often go now, though I'm sorry, and as for converting the child, I never felt clever enough for that. I didn't really try, seemed to me it would be a waste of time with that truculent little thing. Folk set the priest on me once, and he read me a right lecture, but I was putting it off until the child reached the age of reason. Still, I reckon we'll be waiting a long time yet for that, although she's past fifteen years old now, but she's so strange and wilful. Odd folk, these Jews, who knows much about them? Her old grandfather seemed to me a good man, and she's not a bad girl, hard as it is to get close to her. And as for your idea, sir, I like it well enough, I think an honest Christian can never do too much for the salvation of his soul, and everything we do will be judged one day … but I'll tell you straight, I have no real power over the child. When she looks at you with those big black eyes you don't have the heart to do anything that might hurt her. But see for yourself. I'll call her down."

He stood up, poured himself another glass, drained it standing there with his legs apart, and then marched across the tavern to some sailors who had just come in and were puffing at their short-stemmed white clay pipes, filling the place with thick smoke. He shook hands with them in friendly fashion, filled their glasses and joked with them. Then he remembered what he was on his way to do, and the painter heard him make his way up the stairs with a heavy tread.

He felt strangely disturbed. The wonderful confidence he had drawn from that happy moment of emotion on seeing the girl began to cloud over in the murky light of this tavern. The dust of the street and the dark smoke were imposed on the shining image he remembered. And back came his sombre fear that it was a sin to take the solid, animal humanity that could not be separated from earthly women, mingling it with sublime ideas and elevating it to the throne of his pious dreams. He shuddered, wondering from what hands he was to receive the gift to which miraculous signs, both secret and revealed, had pointed his way.

The landlord came back into the tavern, and in his heavy, broad black shadow the painter saw the figure of the girl, standing in the doorway indecisively, seeming to be alarmed by the noise and the smoke, holding the doorpost with her slender hands as if seeking for help. An impatient word from the landlord telling her to hurry up alarmed her, and sent her shrinking further back into the darkness of the stairway, but the painter had already risen to approach her. He took her hands in his—old and rough as they were, they were also very gentle—and asked quietly and kindly, looking into her eyes, "Won't you sit down with me for a moment?"

The girl looked at him, astonished by the kindness and affection in the deep, bell-like sound of his voice on hearing it for the first time there in the dark, smoky tavern. She felt how gentle his hands were, and saw the tender goodness in his eyes with the sweet diffidence of a girl who has been hungering for affection for weeks and years, and is amazed to receive it. When she saw his snow-white head and kindly features, the image of her dead grandfather's face rose suddenly before her mind's eye, and forgotten notes sounded in her heart, chiming with loud jubilation through her veins and up into her throat, so that she could not say a word in reply, but blushed and nodded vigorously—almost as if she were angry, so harshly abrupt was the sudden movement. Timidly, she followed him to his table and perched on the edge of the bench beside him.

The painter looked affectionately down at her without saying a word. Before the old man's clear gaze, the tragic loneliness and proud sense of difference that had been present in this child from an early age flared up suddenly in her eyes. He would have liked to draw her close and press a reassuring kiss of benediction on her brow, but he was afraid of alarming her, and he feared the eyes of the other guests, who were pointing the strange couple out to each other and laughing. Before even hearing a word from this child he understood her very well, and warm sympathy rose in him, flowing freely, for he understood the painful defiance, harsh and brusque and defensive, of someone who wants to give an infinite wealth of love, yet who feels rejected. He gently asked, "What is your name, child?"

She looked up at him with trust, but in confusion. All this was still too strange and alien to her. Her voice shook shyly as she replied quietly, half turning away, "Esther."

The old man sensed that she trusted him but dared not show it yet. He began, in a quiet voice, "I am a painter, Esther, and I would like to paint a picture of you. Nothing bad will happen to you, you will see a great many beautiful things in my studio, and perhaps we will sometimes talk to each other like good friends. It will only be for one or two hours a day, as long as you please and no more. Will you come to my studio and let me paint you, Esther?"

The girl blushed even more rosily and did not know what to say. Dark riddles suddenly opened up before her, and she could not find her way to them. Finally she looked at the landlord, who was standing curiously by, with an uneasy, questioning glance.

"Your father will allow it and likes the idea," the painter made haste to say. "The decision is yours alone, for I cannot and do not want to force you into it. So will you let me paint you, Esther?"

He held out his large, brown, rustic hand invitingly. She hesitated for a moment, and then, bashfully and without a word, placed her own small white hand in the painter's to show her consent. His hand enclosed hers for a moment, as if it were prey he had caught. Then he let it go with a kindly look. The landlord, amazed to see the bargain so quickly concluded, called over some of the sailors from the other tables to point out this extraordinary event. But the girl, ashamed to be at the centre of attention, quickly jumped up and ran out of the door like lightning. The whole company watched her go in surprise.

"Good heavens above," said the astonished landlord, "that was a masterstroke, sir. I'd never have expected that shy little thing to agree."

And as if to confirm this statement he poured another glassful down his throat. The painter, who was beginning to feel ill at ease in the company here as it slowly lost its awe of him, threw some money on the table, discussed further details with the landlord, and warmly shook his hand. However, he made haste to leave the tavern; he did not care for its musty air and all the noise, and the drunk, bawling customers repelled him.

When he came out into the street the sun had just set, and only a dull pink twilight lingered in the sky. The evening was mild and pure. Walking slowly, the old man went home musing on events that seemed to him as strange and yet as pleasing as a dream. There was reverence in his heart, and it trembled as happily as when the first bell rang from the church tower calling the congregation to prayers, to be answered by the bells of all the other towers nearby, their voices deep and high, muffled and joyful, chiming and murmuring, like human beings calling out in joy and sorrow and pain. It seemed to him extraordinary that after following a sober and straightforward path all his life, his heart should be inflamed at this late hour by the soft radiance of divine miracles, but he dared not doubt it, and he carried the grace of that radiance for which he had longed home through the dark streets, blessedly awake and yet in a wonderful dream.

Days had passed by, and still the blank canvas stood on the painter's easel. Now, however, it was not despondency paralysing his hands, but a sure inner confidence that no longer counted the days, was in no hurry, and instead waited in serene silence while he held his powers in restraint. Esther had been timid and shy when she first visited the studio, but she soon became more forthcoming, gentler and less timid, basking in his fatherly warmth as he bestowed it on the simple, frightened girl. They spent these days merely talking to each other, like friends meeting after long years apart who have to get acquainted again before putting ardent feeling into heartfelt words and reviving their old intimacy. And soon there was a secret bond between these two people, so dissimilar and yet so like each other in a certain simplicity—one of them a man who had learnt that clarity and silence are at the heart of life, an experienced man schooled in simplicity by long days and years; the other a girl who had never yet truly felt alive, but had dreamt her days away as if surrounded by darkness, and who now felt the first ray from a world of light reach her heart, reflecting it back in a glow of radiance. The difference between the sexes meant nothing to the two of them; such thoughts were now extinguished in him and merely cast the evening light of memory into his life, and as for the girl, her dim sense of her own femininity had not fully awoken and was expressed only as vague, restless longing that had no aim as yet. A barrier still stood between them, but might soon give way—their different races and religions, the discipline of blood that has learnt to see itself as strange and hostile, nurturing distrust that only a moment of great love will overcome. Without that unconscious idea in her mind the girl, whose heart was full of pent-up affection, would long ago have thrown herself in tears on the old man's breast, confessing her secret terrors and growing longings, the pains and joys of her lonely existence. As it was, however, she showed her feelings only in glances and silences, restless gestures and hints. Whenever she felt everything in her trying to flow towards the light and express itself in clear, fluent words of ardent emotion, a secret power took hold of her like a dark, invisible hand and stifled them. And the old man did not forget that all his life he had regarded Jews if not with hatred, at least with a sense that they were alien. He hesitated to begin his picture because he hoped that the girl had been placed in his path only to be converted to the true faith. The miracle was not to be worked for him; he was to work it for her. He wanted to see in her eyes the same deep longing for the Saviour that the Mother of God must herself have felt when she trembled in blessed expectation of his coming. He would like to fill her with faith before painting a Madonna who still felt the awe of the Annunciation, but had already united it with the sweet confidence of coming fulfilment. And around his Madonna he imagined a mild landscape, a day just before the coming of spring, with white clouds moving through the air like swans drawing the warm weather along on invisible threads, with the first tender green showing as the moment of resurrection approached, flowers opening their buds to announce the coming of blessed spring as if in high, childlike voices. But the girl's eyes still seemed to him too timid and humble. He could not yet kindle the mystic flame of the Virgin's Annunciation and her devotion to a sombre promise in those restless glances; the deep, veiled suffering of her race still showed there, and sometimes he sensed the defiance of the Chosen People at odds with their God. They did not yet know humility and gentle, unearthly love.

With care and caution he tried to find ways to bring the Christian faith closer to her heart, knowing that if he showed it to her glowing in all its brightness, like a monstrance with the sun sparkling in it to show a thousand colours, she would not sink down before it in awe but turn brusquely away, seeing it as a hostile sign. There were many pictures taken from the Scriptures in his portfolios, works painted when he was an apprentice and sometimes copied again later when he was overcome by emotion. He took them out now and looked at the pictures side by side, and soon he felt the deep impression that many of them made on his mind in the trembling of his hands, and the warmth of his breath on his cheeks as it came faster. A bright world of beauty suddenly lay before the eyes of the lonely girl, who for years had seen only the swollen figures of guests at the tavern, the wrinkled faces of old, black-clad women, the grubby children shouting and tussling with each other in the street. But here were gentlewomen of enchanting beauty wearing wonderful dresses, ladies proud and sad, dreamy and desirable, knights in armour with long and gorgeous robes laughing or talking to the ladies, kings with flowing white locks on which golden crowns shone, handsome young men who had suffered martyrdom, sinking to the ground pierced by arrows or bleeding to death under torture. And a strange land that she did not know, although it touched her heart sweetly like an unconscious memory of home, opened up before her—a land of green palms and tall cypress trees, with a bright blue sky, always the same deep hue, above deserts and mountains, cities and distant prospects. Its radiant glow seemed much lighter and happier than this northern sky of eternal grey cloud.

Gradually he began telling her little stories about the pictures, explaining the simple, poetic legends of the Bible, speaking of the signs and wonders of that holy time with such enthusiasm that he forgot his own intentions, and he described, in ecstatic terms, the confidence in his faith that had brought him grace so recently. And the old man's deeply felt faith touched the girl's heart; she felt as if a wonderful country were suddenly revealed to her, opening its gates in the dark. She was less and less certain of herself as her life woke from the depths of the dark to see crimson light. She herself was feeling so strange that nothing seemed to her incredible—not the story of the silver star followed by three kings from distant lands, with their horses and camels bearing bright burdens of precious things—nor the idea that a dead man, touched by a hand in blessing, might wake to life again. After all, she felt the same wonderful power at work in herself. Soon the pictures were forgotten. The old man told her about his own life, connecting the old legends with many signs from God. He was bringing to light much that he had thought and dreamt of in his old age, and he himself was surprised by his own eloquence, as if it were something strange taken from another's hand to be tested. He was like a preacher who begins with a text from the word of God, meaning to explain and interpret it, and who then suddenly forgets his hearers and his intentions and gives himself up to the pleasure of letting all the springs of his heart flow into a deep torrent of words, as if into a goblet containing all the sweetness and sanctity of life. And then the preacher's words rise higher and higher above the heads of the humble members of his congregation, who cannot reach up to the world he now inhabits, but murmur and stare at him as he approaches the heavens in his bold dream, forgetting the force of gravity that will weigh down his wings again …

The painter suddenly looked around him as if still surrounded by the rosy mists of his inspired words. Reality showed him its cold and ordered structure once more. But what he saw was itself as beautiful as a dream.

Esther was sitting at his feet looking up at him. Gently leaning on his arm, gazing into the still, blue, clear eyes that suddenly seemed so full of light, she had gradually sunk down beside him, and in his devout emotion he had never noticed. She was crouching at his knees, her eyes turned up to him. Old words from her own childhood were suddenly present in her confused mind, words that her father, wearing his solemn black robe and frayed white bands, had often read from an old and venerable book. Those words too had been so full of resonant ceremony and ardent piety. A world that she had lost, a world of which she now knew little came back to life in muted colours, filling her with poignant longing and bringing the gleam of tears to her eyes.

When the old man bent down to those sad eyes and kissed her forehead, he felt a sob shaking her tender, childlike frame in a wild fever. And he misunderstood her. He thought the miracle had happened, and God, in a wonderful moment, had given his usually plain and simple manner of speech the glowing, fiery tongue of eloquence as he once gave it to the prophets when they went out to his people. He thought this awe was the shy, still timorous happiness of one who was on her way home to the true faith, in which all bliss was to be found, and she was trembling and swaying like a flame suddenly lit, still feeling its way up into the air before settling into a clear, steady glow. His heart rejoiced at his mistake; he thought that he was suddenly close to his aim. He spoke to her solemnly.

"I have told you about miracles, Esther. Many say that miracles only happened long ago, but I feel and I tell you now that they still happen today. However, they are quiet miracles, and are only to be found in the souls of those who are ready for them. What has happened here is a miracle—my words and your tears, rising from our blind hearts, have become a miracle of enlightenment worked by an invisible hand. Now that you have understood me you are one of us; at the moment when God gave you those tears you became a Christian … "

He stopped in surprise. When he uttered that word Esther had risen from where she knelt at his feet, putting out her hands to ward off the mere idea. There was horror in her eyes, and the angry, wild truculence that her foster father had mentioned. At that moment, when the severity of her features turned to anger, the lines around her mouth were as sharp as the cut of a knife, and she stood in a defensive attitude like a cat about to pounce. All the ardour in her broke out in that moment of wild self-defence.

Then she calmed down. But the barrier between them was high and dark again, no longer irradiated by supernatural light. Her eyes were cold, restless and ashamed, no longer angry, but no longer full of mystic awe; only reality was in them. Her hands hung limp like wings broken in soaring too high. Life was still a mystery of strange beauty to her, but she dared not love the dream from which she had been so shatteringly woken.

The old painter too felt that his hasty confidence had deceived him, but it was not the first disappointment in his long and questing life of faith and trust. So he felt no pain, only surprise, and then again almost joy to see how quickly *she* felt ashamed. He gently took her two childish hands, still feverishly burning as they were. "Esther, your sudden outburst almost alarmed me. But I do not hold it against you … is that what you are thinking?"

Ashamed, she shook her head, only to raise it again next moment. Again her words were almost defiant.

"But I don't want to be a Christian. I don't want to. I—" She choked on the words for some time before saying, in a muted voice. "I … I hate Christians.

I don't know them but I hate them. What you told me about love embracing everything is more beautiful than anything I have ever heard in my life. But the people in the tavern say that they are Christians too, although they are rough and violent. And ... I don't even remember it clearly, it's all so long ago ... but when they talked about Christians at home, there was fear and hatred in their voices. Everyone hated the Christians. I hate them too ... when I was little and went out with my father they shouted at us, and once they threw stones at us. One of the stones hit me and made me bleed and cry, but my father made me go on, he was afraid, and when I shouted for help ... I don't remember any more about all that. Or yes, I do. Our alleys were dark and narrow, like the one where I live here. And only Jews lived there. But higher up, the town was beautiful. I once looked down at it from the top of a house ... there was a river flowing through it, so blue and clear, and a broad bridge over the river with people crossing it in brightly coloured clothes like the ones you showed me in the pictures. And the houses were decorated with statues and with gilding and gable ends. Among them there were tall, tall towers, where bells rang, and the sun shone all the way down into the streets there. It was all so lovely. But when I told my father he ought to go and see the lovely town with me he looked very serious and said, 'No, Esther, the Christians would kill us.' That frightened me ... and ever since then I have hated the Christians."

She stopped in the middle of her dreams, for all around her seemed bright again. What she had forgotten long ago, leaving it to lie dusty and veiled in her soul, was sparkling once again. She was back there walking down the dark alleys of the ghetto to the house she was visiting. And suddenly everything connected and was clear, and she realised that what she sometimes thought was a dream had been reality in her past life. Her words came tumbling out in pursuit of the images hurrying through her mind.

"And then there was that evening ... I was suddenly snatched up out of my bed ... I saw my grandfather, he was holding me in his arms, his face was pale and trembling ... the whole house was in uproar, shaking, there was shouting and noise. Oh, now it's coming back to me. I hear what they were shouting again—it's the others, they were saying, it's the Christians. My father was shouting it, or my mother, or ... I don't remember. My grandfather carried me down into the darkness, through black streets and alleys ... and there was always that noise and the same shouting—the others, the Christians! How could I have forgotten? And then we went away with a man ... when I woke up we were far out in the country, my grandfather and the man I live with now ... I never saw that town again, but the sky was very red back where we had come from ... and we travelled on ... "

Again she stopped. The pictures seemed to be disappearing, getting slowly darker.

"I had three sisters. They were very beautiful, and every evening they came to my bedside to kiss me good-night … and my father was tall, I couldn't reach up to him, so he often carried me in his arms. And my mother … I never saw her again. I don't know what happened to them, because my grandfather looked away and wouldn't tell me when I asked him. And when he died there was no one I dared to ask."

She stopped once more, and a painful, violent sob burst from her throat. Very quietly, she added, "But now I know it all. How could it all be so dark to me? I feel as if my father were standing beside me saying the words he used to say at that time, it is all so clear in my ears. I won't ask anyone again … "

Her words turned to sobs, to silent, miserable weeping that died away in deep, sad silence. Only a few minutes ago life had shown her an enticing image; now it lay dark and sombre before her again. And the old man had long ago forgotten his intention of converting her as he watched her pain. He stood there in silence, feeling as sad himself as if he must sit down and weep with her, for there were some things that he could not put into words, and with his great love of humanity he felt guilty for unknowingly arousing such pain in her. Shuddering, he felt the fullness of blessing and the weight of a burden to be borne, both coming at the same hour; it was as if heavy waves were rising and falling, and he did not know whether they would raise his life or drag it down into the menacing deeps. But wearily, he felt neither fear nor hope, only pity for this young life with so many different paths opening up before it. He tried to find words; but they were all as heavy as lead and had the ring of false coin. What was all they could express, in the face of such a painful memory?

Sadly, he stroked the hair on her trembling head. She looked up, confused and distracted; then mechanically tidied her hair and rose, her eyes wandering this way and that as if getting used to reality again. Her features became wearier, less tense, and there was only darkness now in her eyes. Abruptly, she pulled herself together, and quickly said, to hide the sobs still rising inside her, "I must go now. It's late. And my father is expecting me."

With a brusque gesture of farewell she shook her head, picked up her skirts and turned to leave. But the old man, who had been watching her with his steady, understanding gaze, called after her. She turned back reluctantly, for there were still tears in her eyes. And again the old man took both her hands in his forceful manner and looked at her. "Esther, I know that you want to go now and not come back again. You do not and will not believe me, because a secret fear deceives you."

He felt her hands relax in his gently, softer now. He went on more confidently, "Come back another day, Esther! We will forget all of this, the happy and the sad part of it alike. Tomorrow we will begin on my picture, and I feel as if it will succeed. And don't be sad any more, let the past rest, don't brood on it. Tomorrow we will begin a new work with new hope—won't we, Esther?"

In tears, she nodded. And she went home again, still timid and uncertain, but with a new and deeper awareness of many things.

The old man stayed there, lost in thought. His belief in miracles had not deserted him, but they had seemed more solemn before; were they only a case of a divine hand playing with life? He abandoned the idea of seeing faith in a mystical promise light up a face when perhaps its owner's soul was too desperate to believe. He would no longer presume to bring God and his own ideas to anyone, he would only be a simple servant of the Lord painting a picture as well as he could, and laying it humbly on God's altar as another man might bring a gift. He felt that it was a mistake to look for signs and portents instead of waiting until they were revealed to him in their own good time.

Humbled, his heart sank to new depths. Why had he wanted to work a miracle on this child when no one had asked him to? Wasn't it enough that when his life was taking bleak and meaningless root, like the trunk of an old tree with only its branches aspiring to reach the sky, another life, a young life full of fear, had come to cling trustfully to him? One of life's miracles, he felt, had happened to him; he had been granted the grace to give and teach the love that still burnt in him in his old age, to sow it like a seed that may yet come to wonderful flower. Hadn't life

109

given him enough with that? And hadn't God shown him the way to serve him? He had wanted a female figure in his picture, and the model for it had come to meet him, wasn't it God's will for him to paint her likeness, and not try converting her to a faith that she might never be able to understand? Lower and lower sank his heart.

Evening and darkness came into his room. The old man stood up, feeling a restlessness unusual to him in his late days, for they were usually as mild as cool rays of autumn sunlight. He slowly kindled a light. Then he went to the cupboard and looked for an old book. His heart was weary of restlessness. He took the Bible, kissed it ardently, and then opened it and read until late into the night.

He began work on the picture. Esther sat leaning thoughtfully back in a soft, comfortable armchair, sometimes listening to the old man as he told her all kinds of stories from his own life and the lives of others, trying to while away the monotonous hours of sitting still for her. Sometimes she just sat calmly dreaming in the large room where the tapestries, pictures and drawings adorning the walls attracted her gaze. The painter's progress was slow. He felt that the studies he was doing of Esther were only first attempts, and had not yet caught the final conviction that he wanted. There was still something lacking in the idea behind his sketches; he could not put it into words, but he felt it deep within him so clearly that feverish haste often drove him on from sketch to sketch, and then, comparing them with each other, he was still not content, faithful as his likenesses of Esther were. He did not mention it to the girl, but he felt as if the harsh set of her lips, a look that never entirely left them even when she was gently dreaming, would detract from the serene expectation that was to transfigure his Madonna. There was too much childish defiance in her for her mood to turn to sweet contemplation of motherhood. He did not think any words would really dispel that darkness in her; it could change only from within. But the soft, feminine emotion he wanted would not come to her face, even when the first spring days cast red-gold sunlight into the room through every window and the whole world stirred as it revived, when all colours seemed to be even softer and deeper, like the warm air wafting through the streets. Finally the painter grew weary. He was an experienced old man, he knew the limits of his art, and he knew he could not overcome them by force. Obeying the insistent voice of sudden intuition, he soon gave up his original plan for the painting. And after weighing up the possibilities, he decided not to paint Esther as the Madonna absorbed in thoughts of the Annunciation, since her face showed no signs of devoutly awakening femininity, but as the most straightforward but deeply felt symbol of his faith, the Madonna with her child. And he wanted to begin it at once, because hesitation was making inroads on his soul, again now that the radiance of the miracle he had dreamt of was fading, and had almost disappeared entirely into darkness. Without telling Esther, he removed the canvas, which bore a few fleeting traces of over-hasty sketches, and replaced it with a fresh one as he tried to give free rein to his new idea.

When Esther sat down in her usual way next day and waited, leaning gently back, for him to begin his work— not an unwelcome prospect to her, since it brought inspiring words and happy moments into the bleakness of her lonely day—she was surprised to hear the painter's voice in the next room, in friendly conversation with a woman whose rough, rustic voice she did not recognise. Curious, she pricked up her ears, but she could not hear what they were saying distinctly. Soon the woman's voice died away, a door latched, and the old man came in and went over to her carrying something pale in his arms. She did not realise at once what it was. He carefully placed a small, naked, sturdy child a few months old on her lap. At first the baby wriggled, then he lay still. Esther stared wide-eyed at the old man—she had not expected him to play such a strange trick on her. But he only smiled and said nothing. When he saw that her anxious, questioning eyes were still fixed on him, he calmly explained, in a tone that asked her approval, his intention of painting her with the child on her lap. All the warm kindliness of his eyes went into that request. The deep fatherly love that he had come to feel for this strange girl, and his confidence in her restless heart, shone through his words and even his eloquent silence.

Esther's face had flushed rosy red. A great sense of shame tormented her. She hardly dared to look timidly sideways at the healthy little creature whom she reluctantly held on her trembling knees. She had been brought up among people who had a stern abhorrence of the naked human body, and it made her look at this healthy, happy and now peacefully sleeping baby with revulsion and secret fear; she instinctively hid her own nakedness even from herself, and shrank from touching the little boy's soft, pink flesh as if it were a sin. She was afraid, and didn't know why. All her instincts told her to say no, but she did not want to respond so brusquely to the old man's kindly words, for she increasingly loved and revered him. She felt that she could not deny him anything. And his silence and the question in his waiting glance weighed so heavily on her that she could have cried out with a loud, wordless animal scream. She felt unreasonable dislike of the peacefully slumbering child; he had intruded into her one quiet, untroubled hour and destroyed her dreamy melancholy. But she felt weak and defenceless in the face of the calm old man's kindly wisdom. He was like a pale and lonely star above the dark depths of her life. Once again, as she did in answer to all his requests, she bowed her head in humble confusion.

He said no more, but set about beginning the picture. First he only sketched the outline, for Esther was still far too uneasy and bewildered to embody the meaning of his work. Her dreamy expression had entirely disappeared. There was something tense and desperate in her eyes as she avoided looking at the sleeping, naked infant on her lap, and fixed them instead in endless scrutiny on the walls full of pictures and ornaments to which she really felt indifferent. Her stiff hand showed that she was afraid she might have to bring herself to touch the little body. In addition, the weight on her knees was heavy, but she dared not move. However, the tension in her face showed more and more strongly what a painful effort she was making. In the end the painter himself began to have some inkling of her discomfort, although he ascribed it not to her inherited abhorrence of nakedness but to maidenly modesty, and he ended the sitting. The baby himself went on sleeping like a replete little animal, and did not notice when the painter carefully took him off the girl's lap and put him down on the bed in the next room, where he stayed until his mother, a sturdy Dutch seaman's wife brought to Antwerp for a while by chance, came to fetch him. But although Esther was free of the physical burden she felt greatly oppressed by the idea that she would now have to suffer the same alarm every day.

For the next few days she both came to the studio and left it again uneasily. Secretly, she hoped that the painter would give up this plan as well, and her decision to ask him to do so with a few calm words became compelling and overwhelming. Yet she could never quite bring herself do it; personal pride or a secret sense of shame kept the words back even as they came to her lips like birds ready to take flight. However, as she came back day after day, even though she was so restless, her shame gradually became an unconscious lie, for she had already come to terms with it, as you might come to terms with an unwelcome fact about yourself. She simply did not understood what had happened. Meanwhile the picture was making little progress, although the painter described it cautiously to her. In reality the frame of his canvas contained only the empty and unimportant lines of the figures, and a few fleeting attempts at choosing shades of colour. The old man was waiting for Esther to reconcile herself to his idea, and as his hope that she would verged on certainty he did not try to hurry matters along. For the time being, he made her sittings shorter, and talked a great deal of unimportant matters, deliberately ignoring the presence of the baby and Esther's uneasiness. He seemed more confident and cheerful than ever.

And this time his confidence was well-founded. One morning it was bright and warm, the rectangle of the window framed a light, translucent landscape—towers that were far away, yet the golden gleam on them made them look close; rooftops from which smoke rose in a leisurely fashion, curling up into the deep damask blue of the sky and losing itself there; white clouds very close, as if they were about to descend like downy fluttering birds into the darkly flowing sea of roofs. And the sun cast great handfuls of gold on everything, rays and dancing sparks, circles of light like little clinking coins, narrow strips of it like gleaming daggers, fluttering shapes without any real form that leapt nimbly over the floorboards as of they were bright little animals. This dappled, sparkling play of light had woken the baby from sleep as it tapped at his closed eyelids, until his eyes opened and he blinked and stared. He began moving restlessly on Esther's lap as she reluctantly held him. However, he was not trying to get away from her, only grabbing awkwardly with his clumsy little hands at the sparkling light dancing and playing around them, although he could not seize them, and his failure only made him try harder. His fat little fingers tried to move faster and faster. The sunny light showed the warm flow of blood shining rosily through them, and this simple game made the child's clumsy little body such a charming sight that it cast a spell even on Esther. Smiling with her superior knowledge at the baby's vain attempts to catch and hold the light, she watched his endless game without tiring, quite forgetting her reluctance to hold the innocent, helpless infant. For the first time she felt that there was true human life in the smooth little body—all she had felt before was his naked flesh and the dull satisfaction of his senses—and with childish curiosity of her own she followed all his movements. The old man watched in silence. If he spoke he feared he might revive her truculence and the shame she had forgotten, but his kindly lips wore the satisfied smile of a man who knows the world and its creatures. He saw nothing startling in this change, he had expected and counted on it, confident of the deep laws of nature that never fail. Once again he felt very close to one of those miracles of life that are always renewing themselves, a miracle that can suddenly use children to call forth the devoted kindness of women, and they then give it back to the children, so the miracle passes from being to being and never loses its own childhood but lives a double life, in itself and in those it encounters. And was this not the divine miracle of Mary herself, a child who would never become a woman, but would live on in her child? Was that miracle not reflected in reality, and did not every moment of burgeoning life have about it an ineffable radiance and the sound of what can never be understood?

The old man felt again, deeply, that proximity to the miraculous the idea of which, whether divine or earthly, had obsessed him for weeks. But he knew that he stood outside a dark, closed gate, from which he must humbly turn away again, merely leaving a reverent kiss on the forbidden threshold. He picked up a brush to work, and so chase away ideas that were already lost in clouded gloom. However, when he looked to see how close his copy came to reality, he was spellbound for a moment. He felt as if all his searching so far had been in a world hung about with veils, although he did not know it, and only now that they were removed did its power and extravagance burn before him. The picture he had wanted was coming to life. With shining eyes and clutching hands, the healthy, happy child turned to the light that poured its soft radiance over his naked body. And above that playful face was a second, tenderly bent over the child, and itself full of the radiance cast by that bright little body. Esther held her slender, childish hands on both sides of the baby to protect and avert all misfortune from him. And above her head was a fleeting light caught in her hair and seeming to shine out of it from within. Gentle movement united with moving light, unconsciousness joined dreaming memory, they all came together in a brief and beautiful image, airy and made of translucent colours, an image that could be shattered by a moment's abrupt movement.

The old man looked at the couple as if at a vision. The swift play of light seemed to have brought them together, and as if in distant dreams he thought of the Italian master's almost forgotten picture and its divine serenity. Once again he felt as if he heard the call of God. But this time he did not lose himself in dreams, he put all his strength into the moment. With vigorous strokes, he set down the play of the girl's childish hands, the gentle inclination of her bent head, her attitude no longer harsh. It was as if, although the moment was transitory, he wanted to preserve it for ever. He felt creative power in him like hot young blood. His whole life was in flux and flow, light and colour flowed into that moment, forming and holding his painting hand. And as he came closer to the secret of divine power and the unlimited abundance of life than ever before, he did not think about its signs and miracles, he lived them out by creating them himself.

The game did not last long. The child at last got tired of constantly snatching at the light, and Esther was surprised to see the old man suddenly working with feverish haste, his cheeks flushed. His face showed the same visionary light as in the days when he had talked to her about God and his many miracles, and she felt fervent awe in the presence of a mind that could lose itself so entirely in worlds of creation. And in that overwhelming feeling she lost the slight sense of shame she had felt, thinking that the painter had taken her by surprise at the moment when she was entirely fulfilled by the sight of the child. She saw only the abundance of life, and its sublime variety allowed her to feel again the awe that she had first known when the painter showed her pictures of distant, unknown people, cities as lovely as a dream, lush landscapes. The deprivations of her own life, the monotony of her intellectual experience took on colour from the sound of what was strange and the magnificence of what was distant. And a creative longing of her own burnt deep in her soul, like a hidden light burning in darkness.

That day was a turning point in the history of Esther and the picture. The shadows had fallen away from her. Now she walked fast, stepping lightly, to those hours in the studio that seemed to pass so quickly; they strung together a whole series of little incidents each of which was significant to her, for she did not know the true value of life and thought herself rich with the little copper coins of unimportant events. Imperceptibly, the figure of the old man retreated into the background of her mind by comparison with the baby's helpless little pink body. Her hatred had turned to a wild and almost greedy affection, such as girls often feel for small children and little animals. Her whole being was poured into watching and caressing him; unconsciously and in a passionate game, she was living out a woman's most sublime dream, the dream of motherhood. The purpose of her visits to the studio eluded her. She came, sat down in the big armchair with the healthy little baby, who soon recognised her and would laugh back at her, and began her ardent flirtation with him, quite forgetting that she was here for the sake of the picture, and that she had once felt this naked child was nothing but a nuisance. That time seemed as far away as one of the countless deceptive dreams that she used to spin in her long hours in the dark, dismal alley; their fabric dissolved at the first cautious breath of a wind of reality. Only in those hours at the studio did she now seem to live, not in the time she spent at home or the night into which she plunged to sleep. When her fingers held the baby's plump little hands, she felt that this was not an empty dream. And the smile for her in his big blue eyes was not a lie. It was life, and she drank it in with an avidity for abundance that was a rich, unconscious part of her heritage, and also a need to give of herself, a feminine longing before she was a woman yet. This game already had in it the seed of deeper longing and deeper joy. But it was still only a flirtatious dance of affection and admiration, playful charm and foolish dream. She cradled the baby like a child cuddling her doll, but she dreamt as women and mothers dream—sweetly, lovingly, as if in some boundless distant space.

The old man felt the change with all the fullness of his wise heart. He sensed that he was further from her now, but not stranger, and that he was not at the centre of her wishes but left to one side, like a pleasant memory. And he was glad of this change, much as he also loved Esther, for he saw young, strong, kind instincts in her which, he hoped, would do more than his own efforts to break through the defiance and reserve of the nature she had inherited. He knew that her love for him, an old man at the end of his days, was wasteful, although it could bring blessing and promise to her young life.

He owed wonderful hours to the love for the child that had awakened in Esther. Images of great beauty formed before him, all expressing a single idea and yet all different. Soon it was an affectionate game—his sketches showed Esther playing with the child, still a child herself in her unbounded delight, they showed flexible movements without harshness or passion, mild colours blending gently, the tender merging of tender forms. And then again there were moments of silence when the child had fallen asleep on her soft lap, and Esther's little hands watched over him like two hovering angels, when the tender joy of possession lit in her eyes, and a silent longing to wake the sleeping face with loving play. Then again there were seconds when the two pairs of eyes, hers and the baby's, were drawn to each other unconsciously, unintentionally, each seeking the other in loving devotion. Again, there were moments of charming confusion when the child's clumsy hands felt for the girl's breast, expecting to find his mother's milk there. Esther's cheeks would flush bashfully at that, but she felt no fear now, no reluctance, only a shy surge of emotion that turned to a happy smile.

These days were the creative hours that went into the picture. The painter made it out of a thousand touches of tenderness, a thousand loving, blissful, fearful, happy, ardent maternal glances. A great work full of serenity was coming into being. It was plain and simple—just a child playing and a girl's head gently bending down.

But the colours were milder and clearer than he had ever painted colours before, and the forms stood out as sharply and distinctly as dark trees against the glow of an evening sky. It was as if there must be some inner light hidden in the picture, shedding that secret brightness, as if air blew in it more softly, caressingly and clearly than in any other earthly work. There was nothing supernatural about it, and yet it showed the mystical mind of the man who had created it. For the first time the old man felt that in his long and busy creative life he had always been painting, brushstroke after brushstroke, some being of which he really knew nothing. It was like the old folk tale of the magical imps who do their work in hiding, yet so industriously that people marvel in the morning to see all they did overnight. That was how the painter felt when, after moments of creative inspiration, he stepped back from the picture and looked critically at it. Once again the idea of a miracle knocked on the door of his heart, and this time he hardly hesitated to let it in. For this work seemed to him not only the flower of his entire achievement, but something more distant and sublime of which his humble work was not worthy, although it was also the crown of his artistic career. Then his cheerful creativity would die away and turn to a strange mood when he felt fear of his own work, no longer daring to see himself in it.

So he distanced himself from Esther, who now seemed to him only the means of expressing the earthly miracle that he had worked. He showed her all his old kindness, but once again his mind was full of the pious dreams that he had thought far away. The simple power of life suddenly seemed to him so wonderful. Who could give him answers? The Bible was old and sacred, but his heart was earthly and still bound to this life. Where could he ask whether the wings of God descended to this world? Were there signs of God still abroad today, or only the ordinary miracles of life?

The old man did not venture to wish for the answer, although he had seen strange things during his life. But he was no longer as sure of himself as in the old days when he believed in life and in God, and did not stop to wonder which of them was really true. Every evening he carefully covered up the picture, because once recently, on coming home to see silver moonlight resting on it like a blessing, he felt as if the Mother of God herself had shown him her face, and he could almost have thrown himself down in prayer before the work of his own hands.

Something else, however, happened at this time in Esther's life, nothing in itself strange or unlikely, but it affected the depths of her being like a rising storm and left her trembling in pain that she did not understand. She was experiencing the mystery of maturity, turning from a child into a woman. She was bewildered, since no one had taught her anything about it in advance; she had gone her own strange way alone between deep darkness and mystical light. Now longing awoke in her and did not know where to turn. The defiance that used to make her avoid playing with other children or speaking an unnecessary word burnt like a dark curse at this time. She did not feel the secret sweetness of the change in her, the promise of a seed not yet ready to come to life, only a dull, mysterious pain that she had to bear alone. In her ignorance, she saw the legends and miracles of which the old painter had spoken like lights leading her astray, while her dreams followed them through the most unlikely of possibilities. The story of the mild woman whose picture she had seen, the girl who became a mother after a wonderful Annunciation, suddenly struck her with almost joyful fear. She dared not believe it, because she had heard many other things that she did not understand. However, she thought that some miracle must be taking place inside her because she felt so different in every way, the world and everyone in it also suddenly seemed so different, deeper, stranger, full of secret urges. It all appeared to come together into an inner life trying to get out, then retreating again. There was some common factor at work; she did not know where it lay, but it seemed to hold everything that had once been separate together. She herself felt a force that was trying to take her out into life, to other human beings, but it did not know where to turn, and left behind only that urgent, pressing, tormenting pain of unspent longing and unused power.

In these hours when she was overwhelmed by desperation and needed some kind of support to cling to, Esther tried something that she had thought impossible before. She spoke to her foster father. Until now she had instinctively avoided him, because she felt the distance between them. But now she was driven over that threshold. She told him all about it, and talked about the picture, she looked deep into herself to find something gleaned from those hours that could be useful to her. And the landlord, visibly pleased to hear of the change in her, patted her cheeks with rough kindness and listened. Sometimes he put in a word, but it was as casual and impersonal as the way he spat out tobacco. Then he told her, in his own clumsy fashion, what had just happened to her. Esther listened, but it was no use. He didn't know what else to say to her and didn't even try. Nothing seemed to touch him except outwardly, there was no real sympathy between them, and his words suggested an indifference that repelled her. She knew now what she had only guessed before—people like him could never understand her. They might live side by side, but they did not know each other; it was like living in a desert. And in fact she thought her foster father was the best of all those who went in and out of this dismal tavern, because he had a certain rough plainness about him that could turn to kindness.

However, this disappointment could not daunt the power of her longings, and they all streamed back towards the two living beings she knew who spanned the morning and evening of human life. She desperately counted the lonely night hours still separating her from morning, and then she counted the morning hours separating her from her visit to the painter. Her ardent longings showed in her face. And once out in the street she abandoned herself entirely to her passion like a swimmer plunging into a foaming torrent, and raced through the hurrying crowd, stopping only when, with flushed face and untidy hair, she reached the door of the house she longed to see. In this time of the change in her, she was overcome by an instinctive urge to make free, passionate gestures, and it gave her a wild and desirable beauty.

That greedy, almost desperate need for affection made her prefer the baby to the old man, in whose friendly kindness there was a serenity that rejected stormy passion. He knew nothing about the feminine change in Esther, but he guessed it from her demeanour, and her sudden ecstatic transports made him uneasy. Sensing the nature of the elemental urge driving her on, he did not try to rein it in. Nor did he lose his fatherly love for this lonely child, although his mind had gone back to contemplation of the abstract interplay of the secret forces of life. He was glad to see her, and tried to keep her with him. The picture was in fact finished, but he did not tell Esther so, not wishing to part her from the baby on whom she lavished such affection. Now and then he added a few brushstrokes, but they were minor details—the design of a fold, a slight shading in the background, a fleeting nuance added to the play of light. He dared not touch the real idea behind the picture any more, for the magic of reality had slowly retreated, and he thought the dual aspect of the painting conveyed the spiritual nature of the wonderful creativity that now, as the memory of his execution of it faded, seemed to him less and less like the work of earthly powers. Any further attempt at improvement, he thought, would be not only folly but a sin. And he made up his mind that after this work, in which his hand had clearly been guided, he would do no more paintings, for they could only be lesser works, but spend his days in prayer and in searching for a way to reach those heights whose golden evening glow had rested on him in these late hours of his life.

With the fine instinct that the orphaned and rejected harbour in their hearts, like a secret network of sensitive fibres encompassing everything said and unsaid, Esther sensed the slight distance that the old man who was so dear to her had placed between them, and his mild tenderness, which was still the same, almost distressed her. She felt that at this moment she needed his whole attention and the free abundance of his love so that she could tell him all that was in her heart, all that now troubled it, and ask for answers to the riddles around her. She waited for the right moment to let out the words to express her mental turmoil, but the waiting was endless and tired her out. So all her affection was bent on the child. Her love concentrated on that helpless little body; she would catch the baby up and smother him with warm kisses so impetuously, forgetting his vulnerability, that she hurt him and he began to cry. Then she was less fiercely loving, more protective and reassuring, but even her anxieties were a kind of ecstasy, just as her feelings were not truly maternal, but more of a surge of longing erotic instincts dimly sensed. A force was trying to emerge in her, and her ignorance led her to turn it on the child. She was living out a dream, in a painful dazed state; she clung convulsively to the baby because he had a warm, beating heart, like hers, because she could lavish all the tenderness in her on his silent lips, because with him, unconsciously longing for a human touch, she could clasp another living creature without fearing the shame that came over her if she said a single word to a stranger. She spent hours and hours like that, never tiring, and never realising how she was giving herself away.

For her, all the life for which she longed so wildly was now contained in the child. These were dark times, growing even darker, but she never noticed. The citizens of Antwerp gathered in the evenings and talked of the old liberties and good King Charles, who had loved his land of Flanders so much, with regret and secret anger. There was unrest in the city. The Protestants were secretly uniting. Rabble who feared the daylight assembled, as ominous news arrived from Spain. Minor skirmishes and clashes with the soldiers became more frequent, and in this uneasy, hostile atmosphere the first flames of war and rebellion flared up. Prudent people began to look abroad, others consoled and reassured themselves as well as they could, but the whole country was in a state of fearful expectation, and it was reflected in all faces. At the tavern, the men sat together in corners talking in muted voices, while the landlord spoke of the horrors of war, and joked in his rough way, but no one felt like laughing. The carefree cheerfulness of easy-going folk was extinguished by fear and restless waiting.

Esther felt nothing of this world, neither its muted alarms nor its secret fevers. The child was contented as always, and laughed back at her in his own way—and so she noticed no change in her surroundings. Confused as she was, her life followed a single course. The darkness around her made her fantastic dreams seem real, and it was a reality so distant and strange that she was incapable of any sober, thoughtful understanding of the world. Her femininity, once awakened, cried out for a child, but she did not know the dark mystery involved. She only dreamt a thousand dreams of having a child herself, thinking of the simple marvels of biblical legends and the magical possibility conjured up by her lonely imagination. If anyone had explained this everyday miracle to her in simple words, she might perhaps have looked at the men passing her by with the bashful but considering gaze that was to be seen in the eyes of girls at that time. As it was, however, she never thought of men, only of the children playing in the street, and dreamt of the miracle that might, perhaps, give her a rosy, playful baby some day, a baby all her own who would be her whole happiness. So wild was her wish for one that she might even have given herself to the first comer, throwing aside all shame and fear, just for the sake of the happiness she longed for, but she knew nothing about the creative union of man and woman, and her instincts led her blindly astray. So she returned, again and again, to the other woman's baby. By now she loved him so deeply that he seemed like her own.

One day she came to visit the painter, who had noticed with secret uneasiness her extreme, almost unhealthily passionate love of the child. She arrived with a radiant face and eagerness sparkling in her eyes. The baby was not there as usual. That made her anxious, but she would not admit it, so she went up to the old man and asked him about the progress of his picture. As she put this question the blood rose to her face, for all at once she felt the silent reproach of the many hours when she had paid neither him nor his work any attention. Her neglect of this kindly man weighed on her conscience. But he did not seem to notice.

"It is finished, Esther," he said with a quiet smile. "It was finished long ago. I shall be delivering it tomorrow."

She turned pale, and felt a terrible presentiment that she dared not consider more closely. Very quietly and slowly she asked, "Then I can't come and see you any more?"

He put out both hands to her in the old, warm, compelling gesture that always captivated her. "As often as you like, my child. And the more often that is the happier I shall be. As you see, I am lonely here in this old room of mine, and when you are here it is bright and cheerful all day. Come to see me often, Esther, very often."

All her old love for the old man came welling up, as if to break down all barriers and pour itself out in words. How good and kind he was! Was he not real, and the baby only her own dream? At that moment she felt confident again, but other ideas still hung over that budding confidence like a storm cloud. And the thought of the child tormented her. She wanted to suppress her pain, she kept swallowing the words, but they came out at last in a wild, desperate cry. "What about the baby?"

The old man said nothing, but there was a harsh, almost unsparing expression on his face. Her neglect of him at this moment, when he had hoped to make her soul entirely his own, was like an angry arm warding him off. His voice was cold and indifferent as he said, "The baby has gone away."

He felt her glance hanging on his lips in wild desperation. But a dark force in him made him cruel. He added nothing to what he had said. At that moment he even hated the girl who could so ungratefully forget all the love he had given her, and for a second this kind and gentle man felt a desire to hurt her. But it was only a brief moment of weakness and denial, like a single ripple running away into the endless sea of his gentle kindness. Full of pity for what he saw in her eyes, he turned away.

She could not bear this silence. With a wild gesture, she flung herself on his breast and clung to him, sobbing and moaning. Torment had never burnt more fiercely in her than in the desperate words she cried out between her tears. "I want the baby back, my baby. I can't live without him, they've stolen my one small happiness from me. Why do you want to take the baby away from me? I know I've been unkind to you … Oh, please forgive me and let me have the baby back! Where is he? Tell me! Tell me! I want the baby back … "

The words died away into silent sobbing. Deeply shaken, the old man bent down to her as she clung to him, her convulsive weeping slowly dying down, and she sank lower and lower like a dying flower. Her long, dark hair had come loose, and he gently stroked it. "Be sensible, Esther, and don't cry. The baby has gone away, but—"

"It's not true, oh no, it can't be true!" she cried.

"It *is* true, Esther. His mother has left the country. Times are bad for foreigners and heretics here—and for

133

the faithful and God-fearing as well. They have gone to France, or perhaps England. But why so despairing? Be sensible, Esther, wait a few days and you'll see, you will feel better again."

"I can't, I won't," she cried through more tears. "Why have they taken the baby away from me? He was all I had … I must have him back, I must, I must. He loved me, he was the only creature in the world who was mine, all mine … how am I to live now? Tell me where he is, oh, tell me … "

Her mingled sobs and lamentations became confused, desperate murmuring growing softer and more meaningless, and finally turning to hopeless weeping. Ideas shot like lightning through her tormented mind, She was unable to think clearly and calm down. All she thought and felt circled crazily, restlessly and with pitiless force around the one painful thought obsessing her. The endless silent sea of her questing love surged with loud, despairing pain, and her words flowed on, hot and confused, like blood running from a wound that would not close. The old man had tried to calm her distress with gentle words, but now, in despair, he could say nothing. The elemental force and dark fire of her passion seemed to him stronger than any way he knew of pacifying her. He waited and waited. Sometimes her torrent of feeling seemed to hesitate briefly and grow a little calmer, but again and again a sob set off words that were half a scream, half weeping.

Her young soul, rich with love to give, was bleeding to death in her pain.

At last he was able to speak to Esther, but she wouldn't listen. Her eyes were fixed on a single image, and a single thought filled her heart. She stammered it all out, as if she were seeing hallucinations. "He had such a sweet laugh … he was mine, all mine for all those lovely days, I was his mother … and now I can't have him any more. If only I could see him again, just once … if I could only see him just once." And again her voice died away in helpless sobs. She had slowly slipped down from her resting place against the old man's breast, and was clinging to his knees with weary, shaking hands, crouching there surrounded by the flowing locks of her dark hair. As she stooped down, moving convulsively, her face hidden by her hair, she seemed to be crushed by pain and anger. Monotonously, her desperate mind tiring now, she babbled those words again and again. "Just to see him again … only once … if I could see him again just once!"

The old man bent over her.

"Esther?"

She did not move. Her lips went on babbling the same words, without meaning or intonation. He tried to raise her. When he took her arm it was powerless and limp like a broken branch, and fell straight back again. Only her lips kept stammering, "Just to see him again … see him again, oh, see him again just once … "

At that a strange idea came into his baffled mind as he tried to comfort her. He leant down close to her ear. "Esther? You *shall* see him again, not just once but as often as you like."

She started up as if woken from a dream. The words seemed to flow through all her limbs, for suddenly her body moved and straightened up. Her mind seemed to be slowly clearing. Her thoughts were not quite lucid yet, for instinctively she did not believe in so much happiness revealing itself after such pain. Uncertainly she looked up at the old man as if her senses were reeling. She did not entirely understand him, and waited for him to say more, because everything was so indistinct to her. However, he said nothing, but looked at her with a kindly promise in his eyes and nodded. Gently, he put his arm around her, as if afraid of hurting her. So it was not a dream or a lie spoken on impulse. Her heart beat fast in expectation. Willing as a child, she leant against him as he moved away, not knowing where he was going. But he led her only a few steps across the room to his easel. With a swift movement, he removed the cloth covering the picture.

At first Esther was motionless. Her heart stood still. But then, her glance avid, she ran up to the picture as if to snatch the dear, rosy, smiling baby out of his frame and bring him back to life, cradle him in her arms, caress him, feel the tenderness of his clumsy limbs and bring a smile to his comical little mouth. She did not stop to think that this was only a picture, a piece of painted canvas, only a dream of real life; in fact she did not think at all, she only felt, and her eyelids fluttered in blissful ecstasy. She stood close to the painting, never moving. Her fingers trembled and tingled, longing to feel the child's sweet softness again, her lips burnt to cover the little body with loving kisses again. A fever, but a blessed one, ran through her own body. Then warm tears came to her eyes, no longer angry and despairing, but happy as well as melancholy, the overflowing expression of many strange feelings that suddenly filled her heart and must come out. The convulsions that had shaken her died down, and an uncertain but mild mood of reconciliation enveloped her and gently, sweetly lulled her into a wonderful waking dream far from all reality.

The old man again felt a questioning awe in the midst of his delight. How miraculous was this work that could mysteriously inspire even the man who had created it himself, how unearthly was the sublimity that radiated from it! Was this not like the signs and images of the saints whom he honoured, and who could suddenly make the poor and oppressed forget their troubles and go home liberated and inspired by a miracle? And did not a sacred fire now burn in the eyes of the girl looking at her own portrait without curiosity or shame, in pure devotion to God? He felt that these strange paths must have some destination, there must be a will at work that was not blind like his own, but clear-sighted and master of all its wishes. These ideas rejoiced in his heart like a peal of bells, and he felt he had been touched by the grace of Heaven.

Carefully, he took Esther's hand and led her away from the picture. He did not speak, for he too felt warm tears coming to his eyes and did not want to show them. A warm radiance seemed to rest on her head as it did in the picture of the Madonna. It was as if something great beyond all words was in the room with them, rushing by on invisible wings. He looked into Esther's eyes. They were no longer tearfully defiant, but shadowed only by a gentle reflective bloom. Everything around them seemed to him brighter, milder, transfigured. God's sanctity, miraculously close, was revealing itself to him in all things.

They stood together like that for a long time. Then they began to talk as they used to do, but calmly and sensibly, like two human beings who now understood each other entirely and had no more to search for. Esther was quiet. The sight of the picture had moved her strangely, and made her happy because it restored the happiness of her dearest memory to her, because she had her baby back, but her feelings were far more solemn, deeper and more maternal than they had ever been in reality. For now the child was not just the outward appearance of her dream but part of her own soul. No one could take him away from her. He was all hers when she looked at the picture, and she could see it at any time. The old man, shaken by mystical portents, had willingly answered her desperate request. And now she could feel the same blessed abundance of life every day, her longings need no longer be timid and fearful, and the little childlike figure who to others was the Saviour of the world also, unwittingly, embodied a God of love and life to the lonely Jewish girl.

She visited the studio several more days running. But the painter was aware of his commission, which he had almost forgotten. The merchant came to look at the picture and he too, although he knew nothing about the secret miracles of its creation, was overwhelmed by the gentle figure of the Mother of God and the simple expression of an eternal symbol in its execution. He warmly shook hands with his friend, who, however, turned away his lavish praise with a modest, pious gesture, as if he were not standing in front of his own work. The two of them decided not to keep the altar deprived of this adornment any longer.

Next day the picture occupied the other wing of the altarpiece, and the first was no longer alone. And the pair of Madonnas, strangers but with a slight similarity, were a curious sight. They seemed like two sisters, one of them still confidently abandoning herself to the sweetness of life, while the other had already tasted the dark fruit of pain and knew a terror of times yet to come. But the same radiance hung over both their heads, as if stars of love shone above them, and they would take their path through life with its joy and pain under those stars.

Esther herself followed the picture to church, as if she found her own child there. Gradually the memory that the child was a stranger to her was dying away, and true maternal feelings were aroused in her, making her dream into reality. For hours on end she would lie prostrated before the painting, like a Christian before the image of the Saviour. But hers was another faith, and the deep voices of the bells called the congregation to devotions that she did not know. Priests whose words she could not understand sang, loud choral chanting swept like dark waves through the church, rising into the mystic twilight above the pews like a fragrant cloud. And men and women whose faith she hated surrounded her, their murmured prayers drowning out the quiet, loving words she spoke to her baby. However, she was unaware of any of that. Her heart was too bewildered to look around and take any notice of other people; she merely gave herself up to her one wish, to see her child every day, and thought of nothing else in the world. The stormy weather of her budding youth had died down, all her longings had gone away or had flowed into the one idea that drew her back to the picture again and again, as if it were a magical magnet that no other power could withstand. She had never been so happy as she was in those long hours in the church, sensing its solemnity and its secret pleasures without understanding them. She was hurt only when some stranger now and then knelt in front of the picture, looking adoringly up at the child who was hers, all hers. Then she was defiantly jealous, with anger in her heart that made her want to hit out and shed tears. At such moments her mind was increasingly troubled, and she could not distinguish between the real world and the world of her dreams. Only when she lay in front of the picture again did stillness return to her heart.

Spring passed on, the mild, warm weather in which the picture had been finished still held, and it seemed that after all her stormy suffering, summer too would give her the same great and solemn gift of quiet maternal love. The nights were warm and bright, but her fever had died away, and gentle, loving dreams came over Esther's mind. She seemed to be at peace, rocking to a rhythm of calm passion as the regular hours went by, and all that had been lost in the darkness now pointed her ahead along a bright path into the future.

At last the summer approached its climax, the Feast of St Mary, the greatest day in Flanders. Long processions decked out with pennants blowing in the breeze and billowing banners went through the golden harvest fields that were usually full of busy workers. The monstrance held above the seed corn in the priest's hands as he blessed it shone like the sun, and voices raised in prayer made a gentle sound, so that the sheaves in the fields shook and humbly bowed down. But high in the air clear bells rang in the distance, to be answered joyfully from church towers far away. It was a mighty sound, as if the earth itself were singing together with the woods and the roaring sea.

The glory of the day flowed back from the fertile land into the city and washed over its menacing walls. The noise of craftsmen at work died down, the day labourers' hoarse voices fell silent, only musicians playing fife and bagpipes went from street to street, and the clear silvery voices of dancing children joined the music-making. Silken robes trimmed with yellowing lace, kept waiting in wardrobes all the last year, saw the light of day again, men and women in their best clothes, talking cheerfully, set out for church. And in the cathedral, with its doors open to invite in the pious with clouds of blue incense and fragrant coolness, a springtime of scattered flowers bloomed, pictures and altars were adorned with lavish garlands made by careful hands. Thousands of candles cast magical light into the sweet-scented darkness where the organ roared, and singing, mysterious radiance and mystical twilight reached the heights and depths of the great building.

And then, suddenly a pious and God-fearing mood seemed to flow out into the streets. A procession of the devout formed; up by the main altar the priests raised the famous portrait of St Mary, which seemed to be surrounded by whispered rumours of many miracles, it was borne aloft on the shoulders of the pious, and a solemn procession began. The picture being carried along brought silence to the noisy street, for the crowd fell quiet as people bowed down, and a broad furrow of prayer followed the portrait until it was returned to the cool depths of the cathedral that received it like a fragrant grave.

That year, however, the pious festival was under a dark cloud. For weeks the country had been bearing a heavy burden. Gloomy and as yet unconfirmed news said that the old privileges were to be declared null and void. The freedom fighters known as the Beggars who opposed Spanish rule were making common cause with the Protestants. Dreadful rumours came from the countryside of Protestant divines preaching to crowds of thousands in open places outside the towns and cities, and giving Communion to the armed citizens. Spanish soldiers had been attacked, and churches were said to have been stormed to the sound of the singing of the Geneva Psalms. The was still no definite word of any of this, but the secret flickering of a coming conflagration was felt, and the armed resistance planned by the more thoughtful at secret meetings in their homes degenerated into wild violence and defiance among the many who had nothing to lose.

The festival day had brought the first wave of rioting to Antwerp in the shape of a rabble united in nothing but an instinct to join sudden uprisings. Sinister figures whom no one knew suddenly appeared in the taverns, cursing and uttering wild threats against Spaniards and clerics. Strange people of defiant and angry appearance who avoided the light of day emerged from nooks and crannies and disreputable alleys. There was more and more trouble. Now and then there were minor skirmishes. They did not spill over into a general movement, but were extinguished like sparks hissing out in isolation. The Prince of Orange still maintained strict discipline, and controlled the greedy, quarrelsome and ill-intentioned mob who were joining the Protestants only for the sake of profit.

The magnificence of the great procession merely provoked repressed instincts. For the first time coarse jokes mingled with the singing of the faithful, wild threats were uttered and scornful laughter. Some sang the text of the Beggars' song to a pious melody, a young fellow imitated the croaking voice of the preacher, to the delight of his companions, others greeted the portrait of the Virgin by sweeping off their hats with ostentatious gallantry as if to their lady love. The soldiers and the few faithful Catholics who had ventured to take part in the procession were powerless, and had to grit their teeth and watch this mockery as it became ever wilder. And now that the common people had tasted defiant power, they were becoming less and less amenable. Almost all of them were already armed. The dark impulse that had so far broken out only in curses and threats called for action. This menacing unrest lay over the city like a storm cloud on the feast day of St Mary and the days that followed.

Women and the more sober of the men had kept to their houses since the angry scenes had endangered the procession. The streets now belonged to the mob and the Protestants. Esther, too, had stayed at home for the last few days. But she knew nothing of all these dark events. She vaguely noticed that there were more and more people crowding into the tavern, that the shrill sound of whores' voices mingled with the agitated talk of quarrelling, cursing men, she saw distraught women, she saw figures secretly whispering together, but she felt such indifference to all these things that she did not even ask her foster father about them. She thought of nothing but the baby, the baby who, in her dreams, had long ago become her own. All memory paled beside this one image. The world was no longer so strange to her, but it had no value because it had nothing to give her; her loving devotion and youthful need of God were lost in her thoughts of the child. Only the single hour a day when she stole out to see the picture—it was both her God and her child—breathed real life into her. Otherwise she was like a woman lost in dreams, passing everything else by like a sleepwalker. Day after day, and even once on a long summer night heavy with warm fragrance, when she had fled the tavern and made sure she was shut up in the cathedral, she prostrated herself before the picture on her knees. Her ignorant soul had made a God of it.

And these days were difficult for her, because they kept her from her child. While festive crowds thronged the tall aisles on the Feast of St Mary, and surging organ music filled the nave, she had to turn back and leave the cathedral with the rest of the people crowding it, feeling humbled like a beggar woman because worshippers kept standing in front of the two pictures of St Mary in the chapel that day, and she feared she might be recognised. Sad and almost despairing, she went back, never noticing the sunlight of the day because she had been denied a sight of her child. Envy and anger came over her when she saw the crowds making pilgrimage to the altarpiece, piously coming through the tall porch of the cathedral into that fragrant blue darkness.

She was even sadder next day, when she was not allowed to go out into the streets, now so full of menacing figures. Her room, to which the noise of the tavern rose like a thick, ugly smoke, became intolerable to her. To her confused heart, a day when she could not see the baby in the picture was like a dark and gloomy sleepless night, a night of torment. She was not strong enough yet to bear deprivation. Late in the evening, when her foster father was sitting in the tavern with his guests, she very quietly went down the stairs. She tried the door, and breathed a sigh of relief; it was not locked. Softly, already feeling the mild fresh air that she had missed for a long time, she slipped through the door and hurried to the cathedral.

The streets through which she swiftly walked were dark and full of muffled noise. Single groups had come together from all sides, and news of the departure of the Prince of Orange had let violence loose. Threatening remarks, heard only occasionally and uttered at random in daytime, now sounded like shouts of command. Here and there drunks were bawling, and enthusiasts were singing rebel songs so loud that the windows echoed. Weapons were no longer hidden; hatchets and hooks, swords and stakes glinted in the flickering torchlight. Like a greedy torrent, hesitating only briefly before its foaming waves sweep away all barriers, these dark troops whom no one dared to resist gathered together.

Esther had taken no notice of this unruly crowd, although she once had to push aside a rough arm reaching for her as she slipped by when its owner tried to grab her headscarf. She never wondered why such madness had suddenly come into the rabble; she did not understand their shouting and cries. She simply overcame her fear and disgust, and quickened her pace until at last, breathless, she reached the tall cathedral deep in the shadow of the houses, white moonlit cloud hovering in the air above it.

Reassured, shivering only slightly, she came into the cathedral through a side door. It was dark in the tall, unlit aisles, with only a mysterious silvery light trembling around the dull glass of the windows. The pews were empty. No shadow moved through the wide, breathless expanses of the building, and the statues of the saints stood black and still before the altars. And like the gentle flickering of a glow-worm there came, from what seemed endless depths, the swaying light of the eternal flame above the chapels. All was quiet and sacred here, and the silent majesty of the place so impressed Esther that she muted her tapping footsteps. Carefully, she groped her way towards the chapel in the side aisle and then, trembling, knelt down in front of the picture in boundless quiet rejoicing. In the flowing darkness, it seemed to look down from dense, fragrant clouds, endlessly far away yet very close. And now she did not think any more. As always, the confused longings of her maturing girlish heart relaxed in fantastic dreams. Ardour seemed to stream from every fibre of her being and gather around her brow like an intoxicating cloud. These long hours of unconscious devotion, united with the longing for love, were like a sweet, gently numbing drug; they were a dark wellspring, the blessed fruit of the Hesperides containing and nourishing all divine life. For all bliss was present in her sweet, vague dreams, through which tremors of longing passed. Her agitated heart beat alone in the great silence of the empty church. A soft, bright radiance like misty silver came from the picture, as if shed by a light within, carrying her up from the cold stone of the steps to the mild warm region of light that she knew in dreams. It was a long time since she had thought of the baby as a stranger to her. She dreamt of the God in him and the God in every woman, the essence of her own body, warm with her blood. Vague yearning for the divine, questing ecstasy and the rise of maternal feelings in her spun the deceptive network of her life's dream between them. For her, there was brightness in the wide, oppressive darkness of the church, gentle music played in the awed silence that knew nothing of human language and the passing of the hours. Above her prostrated body, time went its inexorable way.

Something suddenly thudded against the door, shaking it. Then came a second and a third thud, so that she leapt up in alarm, staring into the dreadful darkness. Further thunderous crashing sounds shook the whole tall, proud building, and the isolated lamps rolled like fiery eyes in the dark. Someone was filing through the bolt of the door, now knocked half off its hinges, with a shrill sound like helpless screams in the empty space. The walls flung back the terrifying sounds in violent confusion. Men possessed by greedy rage were hammering at the door, and a roar of excited voices boomed through the hollow shell of the church as if the sea had broken its bounds to come roaring in, and its waves were now beating against the groaning walls of the house of God.

149

Esther listened, distraught, as if woken suddenly from sleep. But at last the door fell in with a crash. A dark torrent of humanity poured in, filling the mighty building with wild bawling and raging. More came, and more. Thousands of others seemed to be standing outside egging them on. Torches suddenly flared drunkenly up like clutching, greedy hands, and their mad, blood-red light fell on wild faces distorted by blind excitement, their swollen eyes popping as if with sinful desires. Only now did Esther vaguely sense the intentions of the dark rabble that she had already met on her way. The first axe-blows were already falling on the wood of the pulpit, pictures crashed to the floor, statues tipped over, curses and derisive cries swirled up out of this dark flood, above which the torches danced unsteadily as if alarmed by such crazy behaviour. In confusion, the torrent poured onto the high altar, looting and destroying, defiling and desecrating. Wafers of the Host fluttered to the floor like white flower petals, a lamp with the eternal flame in it, flung by a violent hand, rushed like a meteor through the dark. And more and more figures crowded in, with more and more torches burning. A picture caught fire, and the flame licked high like a coiling snake. Someone had laid hands on the organ, smashing its pipes, and their mad notes screamed shrilly for help in the dark. More figures appeared as if out of a wild, deranged dream. A fellow with a bloodstained face smeared his boots with holy oil, to the raucous jubilation of the others, ragged

villains strutted about in richly embroidered episcopal
vestments, a squealing whore had perched the golden
circlet from a statue in her tousled, dirty hair. Thieves
drank toasts in wine from the sacred vessels, and up by
the high altar two men were fighting with bright knives
for possession of a monstrance set with jewels. Prostitutes
performed lascivious, drunken dances in front of the
shrines, drunks spewed in the fonts of holy water. Angry
men armed with flashing axes smashed anything within
reach, whatever it was. The sounds rose to a chaotic
thunder of noise and screaming voices; like a dense and
repellent cloud of plague vapours, the crowd's raging
reached to the black heights of the cathedral that looked
darkly down on the leaping flames of torches, and seemed
immovable, out of reach of this desperate derision.

Esther had hidden in the shadow of the altar in the
side chapel, half fainting. It was as if all this must be a
dream, and would suddenly disappear like a deceptive
illusion. But already the first torches were storming into
the side aisles. Figures shaking with fanatical passion as
if intoxicated leapt over gratings or smashed them down,
overturned the statues and pulled pictures off the shrines.
Daggers flashed like fiery snakes in the flickering torchlight, angrily tearing into cupboards and pictures, which
fell to the ground with their frames smashed. Closer and
closer came the crowd with its smoking, unsteady lights.
Esther, breathless, stayed where she was, retreating further into the dark. Her heart missed a beat with alarm and

dreadful anticipation. She still did not know quite what was happening, and felt only fear, wild, uncontrollable fear. A few footsteps were coming closer, and then a sturdy, furious fellow broke down the grating with a blow.

She thought she had been seen. But next moment she saw the intruders' purpose, when a statue of the Madonna on the next altar crashed to the floor in pieces. A terrible new fear came to her—they would want to destroy her picture too, her child—and the fear became certainty when picture after picture was pulled down in the flickering torchlight to the sound of jubilant derision, to be torn and trampled underfoot. A terrible idea flashed through her head—they were going to murder the picture, and in her mind it had long ago become her own living child. In a second everything in her flared up as if bathed in dazzling light. One thought, multiplied a thousand times over, inflamed her heart in that single second. She must save the baby, *her* baby. Then dream and reality came together in her mind with desperate fervour. The destructive zealots were already making for the altar. An axe was raised in the air—and at that moment she lost all conscious power of thought and leapt in front of the picture, arms outstretched to protect it …

It was like a magic spell. The axe crashed to the floor from the now powerless hand holding it. The torch fell from the man's other hand and went out as it fell. The sight struck these noisy, frenzied people like lightning. They all fell silent, except for one in whose throat the gasping cry of "The Madonna! The Madonna!" died away.

The mob stood there white as chalk, trembling. A few dropped to their knees in prayer. They were all deeply shaken. The strange illusion was compelling. For them, there was no doubt that a miracle had happened, one of the kind often authenticated, told and retold—the Madonna, whose features were obviously those of the young mother in the picture, was protecting her own likeness. Pangs of conscience were aroused in them when they saw the girl's face, which seemed to them nothing short of the picture come to life. They had never been more devout that in that fleeting moment.

But others were already storming up. Torches illuminated the group standing there rigid and the girl pressing close to the altar, hardly moving herself. Noise flooded into the silence. At the back a woman's shrill voice cried, "Go on, go on, it's only the Jew girl from the tavern." And suddenly the spell was broken. In shame and rage, the humiliated rioters stormed on. A rough fist pushed Esther aside. She swayed. But she kept on her feet, she was fighting for the picture as if it really were her own warm life. Swinging a heavy silver candlestick, she hit out furiously at the iconoclasts with her old defiance; one of them fell, cursing, but another took his place. A dagger glinted like a short red lightning flash, and Esther stumbled and fell. Already the pieces of the splintered altar were raining down on her, but she felt no more pain. The picture of the Madonna and Child, and the picture of the Madonna of the Wounded Heart both fell under a single furious blow from an axe.

And the raving crowd stormed on; from church to church went the looters, filling the streets with terrible noise. A dreadful night fell over Antwerp. Terror and trembling made its way into houses with the news, and hearts beat in fear behind barred gates. But the flame of rebellion was waving like a banner over the whole country.

The old painter, too, shuddered with fear when he heard the news that the iconoclasts were abroad. His knees trembled, and he held a crucifix in his imploring hands to pray for the safety of his picture, the picture given him by the revelation of God's grace. For a whole wild, dark night dreadful ideas tormented him. And at first light of dawn he could not stay at home any longer.

Outside the cathedral, his last hope faded and fell like one of the overturned statues. The doors had been broken down, and rags and splinters showed where the iconoclasts had been like a bloody trail left behind them. He groped his laborious way through the dark to his picture. His hands went out to the shrine, but they met empty air, and sank wearily to his sides again. The faith in his breast that had sung its pious song in praise of God's grace for so many years suddenly flew away like a frightened swallow.

At last he pulled himself together and struck a light, which flared briefly from his tinder, illuminating a scene that made him stagger back. On the ground, among

154

ruins, lay the Italian master's sweetly sad Madonna, the Madonna of the Wounded Heart, transfixed by a dagger thrust. But it was not the picture, it was the figure of the Madonna herself. Cold sweat stood out on his brow as the flame went out again. He thought this must be a bad dream. When he struck his tinder again, however, he recognised Esther lying there dead of her wound. And by a strange miracle she, who in life had been the embodiment of his own picture of the Virgin, revealed in death the features of the Italian master's Madonna and her bleeding, mortal injury.

Yes, it was a miracle, an obvious miracle. But the old man would not believe in any more miracles. At that hour, when he saw the girl who had brought mild light into the late days of his life lying there dead beside his smashed picture, a string broke in his soul that had so often played the music of faith. He denied the God he had revered for seventy years in a single minute. Could this be the work of God's wise, kind hand, giving so much blessed creativity and bringing splendour into being, only to snatch them back into darkness for no good purpose? This could not be a benign will, only a heartless game. It was a miracle of life and not of God, a coincidence like thousands of others that happen at random every day, coming together and then moving apart again. No more! Could good, pure souls mean so little to God that he threw them away in his casual game? For the first time he stood in a church and doubted

God, because he had thought him good and kind, and now he could not understand the ways of his creator.

For a long time he looked down at the dead girl who had shed such gentle evening light over his old age. And when he saw the smile of bliss on her broken lips, he felt less savage and did God more justice. Humility came back into his kindly heart. Could he really ask who had performed this strange miracle, making the lonely Jewish girl honour the Madonna in her death? Could he judge whether it was the work of God or the work of life? Could he clothe love in words that he did not know, could he reject God because he did not understand his nature?

The old man shuddered. He felt poor and needy in that lonely hour. He felt that he had wandered alone between God and earthly life all these long years, trying to understand them as twofold when they were one and yet defied understanding. Had it not been like the work of some miraculous star watching over the tentative path of this young girl's soul—had not God and Love been at one in her and in all things?

Above the windows the first light of dawn was showing. But it did not bring light to him, for he did not want to see new days dawning in the life he had lived for so many years, touched by its miracles yet never really transfigured by them. And now, without fear, he felt close to the last miracle, the miracle that ceases to be dream and illusion, and is only the dark eternal truth.

DOWNFALL
OF THE HEART

D ESTINY DOES NOT ALWAYS need the powerful prelude of a sudden violent blow to shake a heart beyond recovery. The unbridled creativity of fate can generate disaster from some small, fleeting incident. In clumsy human language, we call that first slight touch the cause of the catastrophe, and feel surprise in comparing its insignificance with the force, often enormous, that it exerts, but just as the first symptoms of an illness may not show at all, the downfall of a human heart can begin before anything happens to make it visible. Fate has been at work within the victim's mind and his blood long before his soul suffers any outward effects. To know yourself is to defend yourself, but it is usually in vain.

The old man—Salomonsohn was his name, and at home in Germany he could boast of the honorary title of Privy Commercial Councillor—was lying awake in the Gardone hotel where he had taken his family for the Easter holiday. A violent physical pain constricted his chest so that he could hardly breathe. The old man was alarmed; he had troublesome gallstones and often suffered bilious attacks, but instead of following the advice of his doctors and visiting Karlsbad to take the waters there he had decided, for his family's sake, to go further south and stay at this resort on Lake Garda instead. Fearing a dangerous attack of his disorder, he anxiously palpated his broad body, and soon realised with relief, even though he was still in pain, that it was only an ordinary stomach upset, obviously as a result of the unfamiliar Italian food, or the mild food poisoning that was apt to afflict tourists. Feeling less alarmed, he let his shaking hand drop back, but the pressure on his chest continued and kept him from breathing easily. Groaning, the old man made the effort of getting out of bed to move about a little. Sure enough, when he was standing the pressure eased, and even more so when he was walking. But there was not much space to walk about in the dark room, and he was afraid of waking his wife in the other twin bed and causing her unnecessary concern. So he put on his dressing gown and a pair of felt slippers, and groped his way out into the corridor to walk up and down there for a little while and lessen the pain.

As he opened the door into the dark corridor, the sound of the clock in the church tower echoed through the open windows—four chimes, first weighty and then dying softly away over the lake. Four in the morning.

The long corridor lay in complete darkness. But from his clear memory of it in daytime, the old man knew that it was wide and straight, so he walked along it, breathing heavily, from end to end without needing a light, and then again and again, pleased to notice that the tightness in his chest was fading. Almost entirely freed from pain now by this beneficial exercise, he was preparing to return to his room when a sound startled him. He stopped. The sound was a whispering in the darkness somewhere near him, slight yet unmistakable. Woodwork creaked, there were soft voices and movements, a door was opened just a crack and a narrow beam of light cut through the formless darkness. What was it? Instinctively the old man shrank back into a corner, not out of curiosity but obeying a natural sense of awkwardness at being caught by other people engaged in the odd activity of pacing up and down like a sleepwalker. In that one second when the light shone into the corridor, however, he had involuntarily seen, or thought he had seen, a white-clad female figure slipping out of the room and disappearing down the passage. And sure enough, there was a slight click as one of the last doors in the corridor latched shut. Then all was dark and silent again.

The old man suddenly began to sway as if he had suffered a blow to the heart. The only rooms at the far end of the corridor, where the door handle had given away a secret by clicking … the only rooms there were his own, the three-roomed suite that he had booked for his family. He had left his wife asleep and breathing peacefully only a few minutes before, so that female figure—no, he couldn't be mistaken—that figure returning from a venture into a stranger's room could have been no one but his daughter Erna, aged only just nineteen.

The old man was shivering all over with horror. His daughter Erna, his child, that happy, high-spirited child—no, this was impossible, he must be mistaken! But what could she have been doing in a stranger's room if not … Like an injured animal he thrust his own idea away, but the haunting picture of that stealthy figure still haunted his mind, he could not tear it out of his head or banish it. He had to be sure. Panting, he groped his way along the wall of the corridor to her door, which was next to his own bedroom. But he was appalled to see, at this one door in the corridor, a thin line of light showing under the door, and the keyhole was a small dot of treacherous brightness. She still had a light on in her room at four in the morning! And there was more evidence—with a slight crackle from the electric switch the white line of light vanished without trace into darkness. No, it was useless trying to pretend to himself. It was Erna, his daughter, slipping out of a stranger's bed and into her own by night.

The old man was trembling with horror and cold, while at the same time sweat broke out all over his body, flooding the pores of his skin. His first thought was to break in at the shameless girl's door and chastise her with his fists. But his feet were tottering beneath the weight of his broad body. He could hardly summon up the strength to drag himself into his own room and back to bed, where he fell on the pillows like a stricken animal, his senses dulled.

The old man lay motionless in bed. His eyes, wide open, stared at the darkness. He heard his wife breathing easily beside him, without a care in the world. His first thought was to shake her awake, tell her about his dreadful discovery, rage and rant to his heart's content. But how could he express it, how could he put this terrible thing into words? No, such words would never pass his lips. What was he to do, though? What *could* he do?

He tried to think, but his mind was in blind confusion, thoughts flying this way and that like bats in daylight. It was so monstrous—Erna, his tender, well-brought-up child with her melting eyes … How long ago was it, how long ago that he would still find her poring over her schoolbooks, her little pink finger carefully tracing the difficult characters on the page, how long since she used to go straight from school to the confectioner's in her little pale-blue dress, and then he felt her childish kiss with sugar still on her lips? Only yesterday, surely? But no, it was all years ago. Yet how childishly she had begged him yesterday—*really* yesterday—to buy her the blue and gold pullover that looked so pretty in the shop window. "Oh please, dear Papa, please!"—with

163

her hands clasped, with that self-confident, happy smile that he could never resist. And now, now she was stealing away to a strange man's bed by night, not far from his own door, to roll about in it with him, naked and lustful.

My God, my God! thought the old man, instinctively groaning. The shame of it, the shame! My child, my tender, beloved child—an assignation with some man … Who is he? Who can he be? We arrived here in Gardone only three days ago, and she knew none of those spruced-up dandies before—thin-faced Conte Ubaldi, that Italian officer, the baron from Mecklenburg who's a gentleman jockey … they didn't meet on the dance floor until our second day. Has one of them already? … No, he can't have been the first, no … it must have begun earlier, at home, and I knew nothing about it, fool that I am. Poor fool! But what do I know about my wife and daughter anyway? I toil for them every day, I spend fourteen hours a day at my office just to earn money for them, more and more money so that they can have fine dresses and be rich … and when I come home tired in the evening, worn out, they've gone gadding off to the theatre, to balls, out with company, what do I know about them and what they get up to all day long? And now my child with her pure young body has assignations with men by night like a common streetwalker … oh, the shame of it!

The old man groaned again and again. Every new idea deepened his wound and tore it open, as if his brain lay visibly bleeding, with red maggots writhing in it.

But why do I put up with this, he wondered, why do I lie here tormenting myself while she, with her unchaste body, sleeps peacefully? Why didn't I go straight into her room so that she'd know *I* knew her shame? Why didn't I beat her black and blue? Because I'm weak … and a coward … I've always been weak with both of them, I've given way to them in everything, I was proud that I could make their lives easy, even if my own was ruined, I scraped the money together with my fingernails, *pfennig* by *pfennig*, I'd have torn the flesh from my hands to see them content! But as soon as I'd made them rich they were ashamed of me, I wasn't elegant enough for them any more, too uneducated … where would I have got an education? I was taken out of school aged twelve, I had to earn money, earn and earn, carry cases of samples about from village to village, run agencies in town after town before I could open my own business … and no sooner were they ladies and living in their own house than they didn't like my honourable old name any more. I had to buy the title of Councillor, so that my wife wouldn't be just Frau Salomonsohn, so that she could be Frau Commercial Councillor and put on airs. Put on airs! They laughed at me when I objected to all that putting on airs of distinction, when I objected to what they call high society, when I told them how my mother, God rest her soul, kept house quietly, modestly, just for my father and the rest of us … they called me old-fashioned. "Oh, you're so old-fashioned, Papa!" She was always mocking

165

me … yes, old-fashioned, indeed I am … and now she lies in a strange bed with strange men, my child, my only child! Oh, the shame, the shame of it!

The old man was moaning and sighing in such torment that his wife, in the bed beside his, woke up. "What's the matter?" she drowsily asked. The old man did not move, and held his breath. And so he lay there motionless in the coffin of his torment until morning, with his thoughts eating away at him like worms.

The old man was first at the breakfast table. He sat down with a sigh, unable to face a morsel of food.

Alone again, he thought, always alone! When I go to the office in the morning they're still comfortably asleep, lazily taking their ease after all their dancing and theatre-going … when I come home in the evening they've already gone out to enjoy themselves in company, they don't need me with them. It's the money, the accursed money that's ruined them, made them strangers to me. Fool that I am, I earned it, scraped it together, I stole from myself, made myself poor and them bad with the money … for fifty pointless years I've been toiling, never giving myself a day off, and now I'm all alone …

He felt impatient. Why doesn't she come down, he wondered, I want to talk to her, I have to tell her … we must leave this place at once … why doesn't she come down? I suppose she's too tired, sleeping soundly with a clear conscience while I'm tearing my heart to pieces, old fool that I am … and her mother titivating herself for hours on end, has to take a bath, dress herself, have a manicure, get her hair arranged, she won't be down before eleven, and is it any wonder? How can a child turn out so badly? It's the money, the accursed money …

Light footsteps were approaching behind him. "Good morning, Papa, did you sleep well?" A soft cheek bent down to his side, a light kiss brushed his hammering forehead. Instinctively he drew back; repelled by the sweetly sultry Coty perfume she wore. And then …

"What's the matter, Papa … are you in a cross temper again? Oh, coffee, please, waiter, and ham and eggs … Did you sleep badly, or have you heard bad news?"

The old man restrained himself. He bowed his head— he did not have the courage to look up—and preserved his silence. He saw only her manicured hands on the table, her beloved hands, casually playing with each other like spoilt, slender little greyhounds on the white turf of the tablecloth. He trembled. Timidly, his eyes travelled up the delicate, girlish arms which she had often—but how long ago?—flung around him before she went to sleep. He saw the gentle curve of her breasts moving in time with her breathing under the new pullover. Naked, he thought grimly, stark naked, tossing and turning in bed with a strange man. A man who touched all that,

167

felt it, lavished caresses on it, tasted and enjoyed her … my own flesh and blood, my child … that villainous stranger, oh …

Unconsciously, he had groaned again. "What's the matter with you, Papa?" She moved closer, coaxing him.

What's the matter with me? echoed a voice inside him. A whore for a daughter, and I can't summon up the courage to tell her so.

But he only muttered indistinctly, "Nothing, nothing!" and hastily picked up the newspaper, protecting himself from her questioning gaze behind a barricade of out-spread sheets of newsprint. He felt increasingly unable to meet her eyes. His hands were shaking. I ought to tell her now, said his tormented mind, now while we're alone. But his voice failed him; he could not even find the strength to look up.

And suddenly, abruptly, he pushed back his chair and escaped, treading heavily, in the direction of the garden, for he felt a large tear rolling down his cheek against his will, and he didn't want her to see it.

The old man wandered around the garden on his short legs, staring at the lake for a long time. Almost blinded by the unshed tears he was holding back, he still could not help noticing the beauty of the landscape—the hills rose in undulating shades of soft green behind silver light, black-hatched with the thin spires of cypress trees, and beyond the hills were the sterner outlines of the mountains, severe, yet looking down on the beauty of the lake without arrogance, like grave men watching the light-hearted games of beloved children. How mild it all lay there outspread, with open, flowering, hospitable gestures. How it enticed a man to be kindly and happy, that timeless, blessed smile of God at the south he had created! Happy! The old man rocked his heavy head back and forth, confused.

One could be happy here, he thought. I would have liked to be happy myself, just once, feel how beautiful the world of the carefree is for myself, just once, after fifty years of writing and calculating and bargaining and haggling, I would have liked to enjoy a few bright days before they bury me ... for sixty-five years, my God, death's hand is in my body now, money is no help and nor are the doctors. I wanted to breathe easily just a little first, have something for myself for once. But my late father always said: contentment is not for the likes of us, we carry our pedlar's packs on our backs to the grave ... Yesterday I thought I myself might feel at ease for a change ... yesterday I could have been called a happy man, glad of my beautiful, lovely child, glad to give her pleasure ... and God has punished me already and taken that away from me. It's all over now for ever ... I can't speak to my own child any more, I am ashamed to look her in the eye. I'll always be thinking of this at home, at the office, at night in my bed—where is she now, where has she been, what has she done? I'll never be able to come happily home again, to see her sitting there and then running to meet me, with my heart opening up at the sight of her, so young and lovely … When she kisses me I'll wonder who had her yesterday, who kissed those lips … I'll always live in fear when she's not with me, I'll always be ashamed when I meet her eyes—a man can't live like this, can't live like this …

The old man stumbled back and forth like a drunk, muttering. He kept staring out at the lake, and his tears ran down into his beard. He had to take off his pince-nez and stand there on the narrow path with his moist, short-sighted eyes revealed, looking so foolish that a gardener's boy who was passing stopped in surprise, laughed aloud and called out a few mocking words in Italian at the bewildered old man. That roused him from his turmoil of pain, and he put his pince-nez on and stole aside into the garden to sit on a bench somewhere and hide from the boy.

But as he approached a remote part of the garden, a laugh to his left startled him again … a laugh that he knew and that went to his heart. That laughter had been music to him for nineteen years, the light laughter of her high spirits … for that laughter he had travelled third-class by night to Poland and Hungary so that he could pour out money before them, rich soil from which that carefree merriment grew. He had lived only for that laughter, while inside his body his gall bladder fell sick … just so that that laughter could always ring out from her beloved mouth. And now the same laughter cut him to the heart like a red-hot saw.

Yet it drew him to it despite his reluctance. She was standing on the tennis court, twirling the racket in her bare hand, gracefully throwing it up and catching it again in play. At the same time as the racket flew up, her light-hearted laughter rose to the azure sky. The three gentlemen admiringly watched her, Conte Ubaldi in a loose tennis shirt, the officer in the trim uniform that showed off his muscles, the gentleman jockey in an immaculate pair of breeches, three sharply profiled, statuesque male figures around a plaything fluttering like a butterfly. The old man himself stared, captivated. Good God, how lovely she was in her pale, ankle-length dress, the sun dusting her blonde hair with liquid gold! And how happily her young limbs felt their own light-ness as she leapt and ran, intoxicated and intoxicating as her joints responded to the free-and-easy rhythm of her movements. Now she flung the white tennis ball merrily up to the sky, then a second and a third after it, it was wonderful to see how the slender wand of her girlish body bent and stretched, leaping up now to catch the last ball. He had never seen her like that before, incandescent with high spirits, an elusive, wavering flame, the silvery trill of her laughter above the blazing of her body, like a virginal goddess escaped in panic from the southern garden with its clinging ivy and the gentle surface of the lake. At home she never stretched that slender, sinewy body in such a wild dance or played competitive games. No, he had never seen her like this within the sombre walls of the crowded city, had never heard her voice rise like lark-song set free from the earthly confines of her throat in merriment that was almost song, not indoors and not in the street. She had never been so beautiful. The old man stared and stared. He had forgotten everything, he just watched and watched that white, elusive flame. And he would have stood like that, endlessly absorbing her image with a passionate gaze, if she had not finally caught the last of the balls she was juggling with a breathless, fluttering leap, turning nimbly, and pressed them to her breast breathing fast, face flushed, but with a proud and laughing gaze. "*Brava, brava!*" cried the three gentlemen, who had been intently watching her clever juggling of the balls, applauding as if she had finished an operatic aria. Their guttural voices roused the old man from his enchantment, and he stared grimly at them.

So there they are, the villains, he thought, his heart thudding. There they are—but which of them is it? Which of those three has had her? Oh yes, how finely rigged out they are, shaved and perfumed, idle dandies … while men like me still sit in offices in their old age, in shabby trousers, wearing down the heels of their shoes visiting customers … and for all I know the fathers of these fine fellows may still be toiling away today, wearing their hands out so that their sons can travel the world, wasting time at their leisure, their faces browned and carefree, their impudent eyes bright. Easy for them to be cheerful, they only have to throw a silly, vain child a few sweet words and she'll fall into bed … But which of the three is it, which is it? One of them, I know, is seeing her naked through her dress and smacking his lips. I've had her, he's thinking, he's known her hot and naked, we'll do it again this evening, he thinks, winking at her—oh, the bastard, the dog, yes, if only I could whip him like a dog!

And now they had noticed him standing there. His daughter swung up her racket in a salutation, and smiled at him, the gentlemen wished him good day. He did not thank them, only stared at his daughter's smiling lips with brimming, bloodshot eyes. To think that you can laugh like that, he thought, you shameless creature … and one of those men may be laughing to himself, telling himself—there goes the stupid old Jew who lies snoring in bed all night … if only he knew, the old fool! Oh yes, I do know, you fine fellows laugh, you tread me underfoot like dirt … but my daughter, so pretty and willing, she'll tumble into bed with you … and as for her mother, she's a little stout now, but she goes about all dolled up with her face painted, and if you were to make eyes at her, who knows, she might yet venture to dance a step or so with you … You're right, you dogs, you're right when they run after you, those shameless women, women on heat … what's it to you that another man's heart is breaking so long as you can have your fun, fun with those shameless females … someone should take a revolver and shoot you down, you deserve to be horsewhipped … but yes, you're right, so long as no one does anything, so long as I swallow my rage like a dog returning to his vomit … you're right, if a father is so cowardly, so shockingly cowardly … if he doesn't go to the shameless girl, take hold of her, drag her away from you … if he just stands there saying nothing, bitter gall in his mouth, a coward, a coward, a coward …

The old man clutched the balustrade as helpless rage shook him. And suddenly he spat on the ground in front of his feet and staggered out of the garden.

The old man made his way unsteadily into the little town. Suddenly he stopped in front of a display window full of all kinds of things for tourists' needs—shirts and nets, blouses and angling equipment, ties, books, tins of biscuits, not in chance confusion but built up into artificial pyramids and colourfully arranged on shelves. However, his gaze went to just one object, lying disregarded amidst this elegant jumble—a gnarled walking stick, stout and solid with an iron tip, heavy in the hand; it would probably come down with a good thump. Strike him down, thought the old man, strike the dog down! The idea transported him into a confused, almost lustful turmoil of feeling which sent him into the shop, and he bought the stout stick quite cheaply. And no sooner was the weighty, heavy, menacing thing in his hand than he felt stronger. A weapon always makes the physically weak more sure of themselves. It was as if the handle of the stick tensed and tautened his muscles. "Strike him down … strike the dog down!" he muttered to himself, and unconsciously his heavy, stumbling gait turned to a firmer, more upright, faster rhythm. He walked, even ran up and down the path by the shores of the lake, breathing hard and sweating, but more from the passion spreading through him than because of his accelerated pace. For his hand was clutching the heavy handle of the stick more and more tightly.

Armed with this weapon, he entered the blue, cool shadows of the hotel lobby, his angry eyes searching for the invisible enemy. And sure enough, there in the corner they were sitting together on comfortable wicker chairs, drinking whisky and soda through straws, talking cheerfully in idle good fellowship—his wife, his daughter and the inevitable trio of gentlemen. Which of them is it, he wondered, which of them is it? And his fist clenched around the handle of the heavy stick. Whose skull do I smash in, whose, whose? But Erna, misunderstanding his restless, searching glances, was already jumping up and running to him. "So here you are, Papa! We've

175

been looking for you everywhere. Guess what, Baron von Medwitz is going to take us for a drive in his Fiat, we're going to drive all along the lake to Desenzano!" And she affectionately led him to their table, as if he ought to thank the gentlemen for the invitation.

They had risen politely and were offering him their hands. The old man trembled. But the girl's warm presence, placating him, lay soft and intoxicating against his arm. His will was paralysed as he shook the three hands one by one, sat down in silence, took out a cigar and bit grimly into the soft end of it. Above him, the casual conversation went on, in French, with much high-spirited laughter from several voices.

The old man sat there, silent and hunched, biting the end of his cigar until his teeth were brown with tobacco juice. They're right, he thought, they're right, I deserve to be spat at … now I've shaken their hands! Shaken hands with all three, and I know that one of them's the villain. Here I am sitting quietly at the same table with him, and I don't strike him down, no, I don't strike him down, I shake hands with him civilly … they're right, quite right if they laugh at me … and see the way they talk, ignoring me as if I weren't here at all! I might already be underground … and they both know, Erna and my wife, that I don't understand a word of French. They both know that, both of them, but no one asked me whether I minded, if only for form's sake, just because I sit here so foolishly, feeling so ridiculous. I might be thin air to them, nothing but thin air, a nuisance, a hanger-on, something in the way of their fun … someone to be ashamed of, they tolerate me only because I make so much money. Money, money, always that wretched, filthy lucre, the money I've spent indulging them, money with God's curse on it. They don't say a word to me, my wife, my own child, they talk away to these idlers, their eyes are all for those smooth, smartly rigged-out dandies … see how they smile at those fine gentlemen, it tickles their fancy, as if they felt their hands on bare female flesh. And I put up with it all. I sit here listening to their laughter, I don't understand what they say, and yet I sit here instead of striking out with my fists, thrashing them with my stick, driving them apart before they begin coupling before my very eyes. I let it all pass … I sit here silent, stupid, a coward, coward, coward …

"Will you allow me?" asked the Italian officer, in laborious German, reaching for his lighter.

Startled out of his heated thoughts, the old man sat up very erect and stared grimly at the unsuspecting young officer. Anger was seething inside him. For a moment his hand clutched the handle of the stick convulsively. But then he let the corners of his mouth turn down again, stretching it into a senseless grin. "Oh, I'll allow you!" he sardonically repeated. "To be sure I'll allow you, ha ha, I'll allow you anything you want—ha ha!—anything I have is entirely at your disposal … you can do just as you like."

The bewildered officer stared at him. With his poor command of German, he had not quite understood, but that wry, grinning smile made him uneasy. The gentleman jockey from Germany sat up straight, startled, the two women went white as a sheet—for a split second the air among them all was breathless and motionless, as electric as the tiny pause between a flash of lightning and the thunder that follows.

But then the fierce distortion of his face relaxed, the stick slid out of his clutch. Like a beaten dog, the old man retreated into his own thoughts and coughed awkwardly, alarmed by his own boldness. Trying to smooth over the embarrassing tension, Erna returned to her light conversational tone, the German baron replied, obviously anxious to maintain the cheerful mood, and within a few minutes the interrupted tide of words was in full flow once more.

The old man sat among the others as they chattered, entirely withdrawn; and you might have thought he was asleep. His heavy stick, now that the clutch of his hands was relaxed, dangled useless between his legs. His head, propped on one hand, sank lower and lower. But no one paid him any more attention, the wave of chatter rolled over his silence, sometimes laughter sprayed up, sparkling, at a joking remark, but he was lying motionless below it all in endless darkness, drowned in shame and pain.

The three gentlemen rose to their feet, Erna followed readily, her mother more slowly; in obedience to someone's light-hearted suggestion they were going into the music room next door, and did not think it necessary to ask the old man drowsing away there to come with them. Only when he suddenly became aware of the emptiness around him did he wake, like a sleeping man roused by the cold when his blanket has slipped off the bed in the night, and cold air blows over his naked body. Instinctively his eyes went to the chairs they had left, but jazzy music was already coming from the room next door, syncopated and garish. He heard laughter and cries of encouragement. They were dancing next door. Yes, dancing, always dancing, they could do that all right! Always stirring up the blood, always rubbing avidly against each other, chafing until the dish was cooked and ready. Dancing in the evening, at night, in bright daylight, idlers, gentlemen of leisure with time on their hands, that was how they charmed the women.

Bitterly, he picked up his stout stick again and dragged himself after them. At the door he stopped. The German baron, the gentleman jockey, was sitting at the piano, half turned away from the keyboard so that he could watch the dancers at the same time as he rattled out an American hit song on the keys, a tune he obviously knew more or less by heart. Erna was dancing with the officer; the long-legged Conte Ubaldi was rhythmically pushing her strong, sturdy mother forward and back, not without

179

some difficulty. But the old man had eyes for no one but Erna and her partner. How that slender greyhound of a man laid his hands, soft and flattering, on her delicate shoulders, as if she belonged to him entirely! How her body, swaying, following his lead, pressed close to his, as if promising herself, how they danced, intertwined, before his very eyes, with passion that they had difficulty in restraining! Yes, he was the man—for in those two bodies moving as one there burnt a sense of familiarity, something in common already in their blood. He was the one—it could only be he, he read it from her eyes, half-closed and yet brimming over, in that fleeting, hovering movement reflecting the memory of lustful moments already enjoyed—he was the man, he was the thief who came by night to seize and ardently penetrate what his child, his own child, now concealed in her thin, semi-transparent, flowing dress! Instinctively he stepped closer to tear her away from the man. But she didn't even notice him. With every movement of the rhythm, giving herself up to the guiding touch of the dancer, the seducer leading her, with her head thrown back and her moist mouth open, she swayed softly to the beat of the music, with no sense of space or time or of the man, the trembling, panting old man who was staring at her in a frenzied ecstasy of rage, his eyes bloodshot. She felt only herself, her own young limbs as she unresistingly followed the syncopation of the breathlessly swirling dance music. She felt only herself, and the fact that a male creature so close to her desired her, his strong arm surrounded her, and she must preserve her balance and not fall against him with greedy lips, hotly inhaling his breath as she abandoned herself to him. And all this was magically known to the old man in his own blood, his own shattered being—always, whenever the dance swept her away from him, he felt as if she were sinking for ever.

Suddenly, as if the string of an instrument had broken, the music stopped in the middle of a bar. The German baron jumped up. "*Assez joué pour vous*," he laughed. "*Maintenant je veux danser moi-même.*"—"You've had your fun. Now I want to dance myself!" They all cheerfully agreed, the group stopped dancing in couples and moved into an informal, fluttering dance all together.

The old man came back to his senses—how he wanted to do something now, say something! Not just stand about so foolishly, so pitifully superfluous! His wife was dancing by, gasping slightly from exertion but warm with contentment. Anger brought him to a sudden decision. He stepped into her path. "Come with me," he said brusquely. "I have to talk to you."

She looked at him in surprise. Little beads of sweat moistened his pale brow, his eyes were staring wildly around. What did he want? Why disturb her just now? An excuse was already forming on her lips, but there was something so convulsive, so dangerous in his demeanour that, suddenly remembering the grim outburst over the lighter just now, she reluctantly followed him.

181

"*Excusez, messieurs, un instant!*" she said, turning back apologetically to the gentlemen. So she'll apologise to *them*, thought the agitated old man grimly, she didn't apologise to me when she got up from the table. I'm no more than a dog to her, a doormat to be trodden on. But they're right, oh yes, they're right if I put up with it.

She was waiting, her eyebrows sternly raised; he stood before her, his lip quivering, like a schoolboy facing his teacher.

"Well?" she finally asked.

"I don't want … I don't want … " he stammered awkwardly. "I don't want you—you and Erna—I don't want you mixing with those people."

"With what people?" Deliberately pretending not to understand, she looked up indignantly, as if he had insulted her personally.

"With those men in there." Angrily, he jerked his chin in the direction of the music room. "I don't like it … I don't want you to … "

"And why not, may I ask?"

Always that inquisitorial tone, he thought bitterly, as if I were a servant. Still more agitated, he stammered, "I have my reasons … I don't like it. I don't want Erna talking to those men. I don't have to tell you everything."

"Then I'm sorry," she said, flaring up, "but I consider all three gentlemen extremely well-brought up, far more distinguished company than we keep at home."

"Distinguished company! Those idlers, those ... those ... " Rage was throttling him more intolerably than ever. And suddenly he stamped his foot. "I don't want it, I forbid it! Do you understand that?"

"No," she said coldly. "I don't understand any of what you say. I don't know why I should spoil the girl's pleasure ... "

"Her pleasure ... her pleasure!" He was staggering as if under a heavy blow, his face red, his forehead streaming with sweat. His hand groped in the air for his heavy stick, either to support himself or to hit out with it. But he had left it behind. That brought him back to his senses. He forced himself to keep calm as a wave of heat suddenly passed over his heart. He went closer to his wife, as if to take her hand. His voice was low now, almost pleading. "You ... you don't understand. It's not for myself ... I'm begging you only because ... it's the first thing I've asked you for years, let's go away from here. Just away, to Florence, to Rome, anywhere you want, I don't mind. You can decide it all, just as you like. I only want to get away from here, please, away ... away, today, this very day. I ... I can't bear it any longer, I can't."

"Today?" Surprised, dismissively, she frowned. "Go away today? What a ridiculous idea! Just because you don't happen to like those gentlemen. Well, you don't have to mingle with them."

He was still standing there, hands raised pleadingly. "I can't bear it, I told you ... I can't, I can't. Don't ask me any more, please ... but believe me, I can't bear it, I can't. Do this for me, just for once, do something for me ... "

In the music room someone had begun hammering at the piano again. She looked up, touched by his cry despite herself, but how very ridiculous he looked, that short fat man, his face red as if he had suffered a stroke, his eyes wild and swollen, his hands emerging from sleeves too short for him and trembling in the air. It was embarrassing to see him standing there in such a pitiful state. Her milder feelings froze.

"That's impossible," she informed him. "We've agreed to go out for that drive today, and as for leaving tomorrow when we've booked for three weeks ... why, we'd make ourselves look ridiculous. I can't see the faintest reason for leaving early. I am staying here, and so is Erna, we are not—"

"And I can go, you're saying? I'm only in the way here, spoiling your ... pleasure."

With that sombre cry he cut her short in mid-sentence. His hunched, massive body had reared up, he had clenched his hands into fists, a vein was trembling alarmingly on his forehead in anger. He wanted to get something else out, a word or a blow. But he turned abruptly, stumbled to the stairs, moving faster and faster on his heavy legs, and hurried up them like a man pursued.

Gasping, the old man went hastily up the stairs; he wanted only to be in his room now, alone, try to control himself, take care not to do anything silly! He had already reached the first floor when—there it came, the pain, as if a burning claw were tearing open his guts from the inside. He suddenly stumbled back against the wall, white as a sheet. Oh, that raging, burning pain kneading away at him; he had to grit his teeth to keep himself from crying out loud. Groaning, his tormented body writhed.

He knew at once what was wrong—it was his gall bladder, one of those fearful attacks that had often plagued him recently, but had never before tortured him so cruelly. Next moment, in the middle of his pain, he remembered that the doctor had prescribed 'no agitation'. Through the pain he grimly mocked himself. Easily said, he thought, no agitation—my dear good Professor, can you tell me how to avoid agitation when … oh, oh …

The old man was whimpering as the invisible, red-hot claw worked away inside his poor body. With difficulty, he dragged himself to the door of the sitting room of the suite, pushed it open, and fell on the ottoman, stuffing the cushions into his mouth. As he lay there the pain immediately lessened slightly; the hot nails of that claw were no longer reaching so infernally deep into his sore guts. I ought to make myself a compress, he remembered, I must take those drops, then it will soon be better.

But there was no one there to help him, no one. And he himself had no strength to drag himself into the next room, or even reach the bell.

There's no one here, he thought bitterly, I shall die like a dog sooner or later, because I know what it is that hurts, it's not my gall bladder, it's Death growing in me. I know it, I'm a defeated man, no professors, no drinking the waters at spas can help me … you don't recover from this sort of thing, not at sixty-five. I know what's piercing me and tearing me from the inside, it's Death, and the few years I have left will not be life, just dying, dying. But when did I ever really live? Live my own life, for myself? What kind of life have I had, scraping money together all the time, always for other people, and now, what help is it to me now? I've had a wife, I married her as a girl, I knew her body and she bore me a child. Year after year we lay together in the same bed … and now, where is she now? I don't recognise her face any more … she speaks so strangely to me, and never thinks of my life, of all I feel and think and suffer … she's been a stranger to me for years now … Where has my life gone, where did it go? … And I had a child, watched her grow up, I thought I'd begin to live again through her, a brighter, happier life than was granted to me, in her I wouldn't entirely die … and now she steals away by night to throw herself at men. There's only me, I shall die alone, all alone … I'm already dead to those two. My God, my God, I was never so much alone …

The claw sometimes closed grimly inside him and then let go again. But another pain was hammering deeper and deeper into his temples; his thoughts, harsh, sharp, were like mercilessly hot gravel in his forehead, he mustn't think just now, mustn't think! The old man had torn open his jacket and waistcoat—his bloated body quivered, plump and shapeless, under his billowing shirt. Cautiously he pressed his hand to the painful place. All that hurts there is me, he felt, it's only me, only this piece of hot skin … and only what's clawing around in it there still belongs to me, it is *my* illness, *my* death … I am all it is … I am not a Privy Commercial Councillor any more, with a wife and child and money and a house and a business … this is all I really am, what I feel with my fingers, my body and the heat inside it hurting me. Everything else is folly, makes no sense now … because what hurts in there hurts only me, what concerns me concerns me alone. They don't understand me any more, and I don't understand them … you are all alone with yourself in the end. I never felt it so much before … But now I know, now I lie here feeling Death under my skin, too late now in my sixty-fifth year, just before dying, now while they dance and go for walks or drift aimlessly about, those shameless women … now I know it, I lived only for them, not that they thank me for it, and never for myself, not for an hour. But what do I care for them now … what do I care for them … why think of them when they never think of me? Better die than accept their pity … what do I care for them now? …

Gradually receding, the pain ebbed away; the cruel hand did not grasp into the suffering man with such red-hot claws. But it left behind a dull, sombre feeling, barely perceptible as pain now, yet something alien pressing and pushing, tunnelling away inside him. The old man lay with his eyes closed, attending carefully to this soft pushing and pulling; he felt as if a strange, unknown power were hollowing something out in him, first with sharp tools, then with blunter ones. It was like something coming adrift, fibre by fibre, within his body. The tearing was not so fierce now, and did not hurt any more. But there was something quietly smouldering and rotting inside him, something beginning to die. All he had lived through, all he had loved, was lost in that slowly consuming flame, burning black before it fell apart, crumbling and charred, into the lukewarm mire of indifference. Something was happening, he knew it vaguely, something was happening while he lay like this, reflecting passionately on his life. Something was coming to an end. What was it? He listened and listened to what was going on inside him.

And slowly his heart began to fail him.

The old man lay in the twilight of the room with his eyes closed. He was still half awake, half already dreaming. And then, between sleeping and waking, it seemed to him in the confusion of his feelings as if, from somewhere or other, something moist and hot was seeping softly into him from a wound that did not hurt and that he was unaware of having suffered. It was like being drained of his own blood. It did not hurt, that invisible flow, it did not run very strongly. The drops fell only slowly, like warm tears trickling down, and each of them struck him in the middle of the heart. But his heart, his dark heart, made no sound and quietly soaked up that strange torrent. Soaked it up like a sponge, became heavier and heavier with it, his heart was already swelling with it, brimming over, it was spilling into the narrow frame of his chest. Gradually filling up, overflowing with its own weight, whatever it was began gently pulling to expand itself, pulling at taut muscles, pressing harder and harder and forcing his painful heart, gigantic by now, down after its own weight. And now (oh, how this hurt!) now the weight came loose from the fibres of flesh—very slowly, not like a stone or a falling fruit, no, like a sponge soaked with moisture it sank deeper and ever deeper into a warm void, down into something without being that was outside himself, into vast and endless night. All at once it was terribly still in the place where that warm, brimming heart had been a moment ago. What yawned

189

empty there now was uncanny and cold. No sensation of thudding any more, no dripping now, all was very still and perfectly dead inside him. And his shuddering breast surrounded that silent and incomprehensible void like a hollow black coffin.

So strong was this dreamlike feeling, so deep his confusion, that when the old man began to wake he instinctively put his hand to the left side of his chest to see whether his heart was still here. But thank God, he felt a pulse, a hollow, rhythmical pulse beating below his groping fingers, and yet it might have been beating mutely in a vacuum, as if his heart was really gone. For strange to say, it suddenly seemed as if his body had left him of its own accord. No pain wrenched at it any more, no memory twitched painfully, all was silent in there, fixed and turned to stone. What's this, he wondered, when just now I felt such pain, such hot pressure, when every fibre was twitching? What has happened to me? He listened, as if to the sounds in a cavern, to find out whether what had been there before was still moving. But those rushing sounds, the dripping, the thudding, they were far away. He listened and listened, no echo came, none at all. Nothing hurt him any more, nothing was swelling up to torment him; it must be as empty and black in there as a hollow, burnt-out tree. And all at once he felt as if he had already died, or something in him had died, his blood was so sluggish and silent. His own body lay under him cold as a corpse, and he was afraid to feel it with his warm hand.

There in his room the old man, listening to what was happening to him, did not hear the sound of church clocks down by the lake striking the hours, each hour bringing deeper twilight. The night was already gathering around him, darkness fell on the things in the room as it flowed away into the night, at last even the pale sky visible in the rectangle of the window was immersed in total darkness. The old man never noticed, but only stared at the blackness in himself, listening to the void there as if to his own death.

Then, at last, there was exuberant laughter in the room next door. A switch was pressed, and light came through the crack of the doorway, for the door was only ajar. The old man roused himself with a start—his wife, his daughter! They would find him here on the day bed and ask questions. He hastily buttoned up his jacket and waistcoat; why should they know about the attack he had suffered, what business of theirs was it?

But the two women had not come in search of him. They were obviously in a hurry; the imperious gong was striking for the third time. They seemed to be dressing for dinner; listening, he could hear every movement through the half-open doorway. Now they were opening the shutters, now they were putting their rings down on the washstand with a light chink, now shoes were tapping on the floor, and from time to time they talked to each other. Every word, every syllable came to the old man's ears with cruel clarity. First they talked about the gentlemen, mocking them a little, about a chance incident on the drive, light, inconsequent remarks as they washed and moved around, dressing and titivating themselves. Then, suddenly, the conversation turned to him.

"Where's Papa?" Erna asked, sounding surprised that he had occurred to her so late.

"How should I know?" That was her mother's voice, instantly irritated by the mere mention of him. "Probably waiting for us down in the lobby, reading the stock prices in the Frankfurt newspaper for the hundredth time—they're all he's interested in. Do you think he's even looked at the lake? He doesn't like it here, he told me so at mid-day. He wanted us to leave today."

"Leave today? But why?" Erna's voice again.

"I really don't know. Who can tell what he has in mind? He doesn't like the other guests here, the company of those gentlemen doesn't suit him—probably he feels how little his company suits them. Really, the way he goes around here is disgraceful, with his clothes all crumpled, his collar open ... you should suggest that he might look a little more *soigné*, at least in the evenings, he'll listen to you. And this morning … I thought I'd sink into the ground to hear him flare up at the lieutenant when he wanted to borrow Papa's lighter."

"Yes, Mama, what was that all about? I wanted to ask you, what was the matter with Papa? I've never seen him like that before … I was really shocked."

"Oh, he was just in a bad temper. I expect prices on the stock exchange have fallen. Or perhaps it was because we were speaking French. He can't bear other people to have a nice time. You didn't notice, but while we were dancing he was standing at the door of the music room like a murderer lurking behind a tree. Leave today! Leave on the spot! Just because that's what he suddenly feels like doing. Well, if he doesn't like it here, there's no need for him to grudge us our pleasure … but I'm not going to bother with his whims any more, whatever he says and does."

The conversation ended. Obviously they had finished dressing for dinner. Yes, the door was opened, they were leaving the room, he heard the click of the switch, and the light went out.

The old man sat perfectly still on the ottoman. He had heard every word. But strange to say, it no longer hurt, it did not hurt at all. The clockwork in his breast that had been hammering and tearing at him fiercely not so long ago had come to a standstill; it must be broken. He had felt no reaction to the sharp touch of their remarks. No anger, no hatred … nothing, nothing.

Calmly, he buttoned up his clothes, cautiously made his way downstairs, and sat down at the dinner table with them as if they were strangers.

He did not speak to them that evening, and for their part they did not notice his silence, which was as concentrated as a clenched fist. After dinner he went back to his room, again without a word, lay down on the bed and put out the light. Only much later did his wife come up from the evening's cheerful entertainment, and thinking he was asleep she undressed in the dark. Soon he heard her heavy, easy breathing.

The old man, alone with himself, stared open-eyed at the endless void of the night. Beside him something lay in the dark, breathing deeply; he made an effort to remember that the body drawing in the same air in the same room was the woman whom he had known when she was young and ardent, who had borne him a child, a body bound to him through the deepest mystery of the blood; he kept forcing himself to think that the warm, soft body there—he had only to put out a hand to touch it—had once been a life that was part of his own. But strangely, the memory aroused no feelings in him any more. And he heard her regular breathing only like the murmuring of little waves coming through the open window as they broke softly on the pebbles near the shore. It was all far away and unreal, something strange was lying beside him only by chance—it was over, over for ever.

Once he found himself trembling very slightly, and stole to his daughter's door. So she was out of her room again tonight. He did feel a small, sharp pang in the heart he had thought dead. For a second, something twitched there like a nerve before it died away entirely. That was over now as well. Let her do as she likes, he thought, what is it to me?

And the old man lay back on his pillow again. Once more the darkness closed in on his aching head, and that cool, blue sensation seeped into his blood—a beneficial feeling. Soon light slumber cast its shadow over his exhausted senses.

When his wife woke up in the morning she saw her husband already in his coat and hat. "What are you doing?" she asked, still drowsy from sleep.

The old man did not turn around. He was calmly packing his night things in a small suitcase. "You know what I'm doing. I'm going home. I'm taking only the necessities; you can have the rest sent after me."

His wife took fright. What was all this? She had never heard his voice like that before, bringing each word out cold and hard. She swung both legs out of bed. "You're not going away, surely? Wait … we'll come with you, I've already told Erna that … "

He only waved this vigorously away. "No, no, don't let it disturb you." And without looking back he made his way to the door. He had to put the suitcase down on the floor for a moment in order to press down the door handle. And in that one fitful second a memory came back—a memory of thousands of times when he had put down his case of samples like that as he left the doors of strangers with a servile bow, ingratiating himself with an eye to further business. But he had no business here and now, so he omitted any greeting. Without a look or a word he picked up his suitcase again and closed the door firmly between himself and his old life.

Neither mother nor daughter understood what had happened. But the strikingly abrupt and determined nature of his departure made them both uneasy. They wrote to him back at home in south Germany at once, elaborately explaining that they assumed there had been some misunderstanding, writing almost affectionately, asking with concern how his journey had been, and whether he had arrived safely. Suddenly compliant, they expressed themselves ready and willing to break off their holiday at any time. There was no reply. They wrote again, more urgently, they sent telegrams, but there was still no reply. Only the sum of money that they had said they needed in one of the letters arrived—a postal remittance bearing the stamp of his firm, without a word or greeting of his own.

Such an inexplicable and oppressive state of affairs made them bring their own return home forward. Although they had sent a telegram in advance, there was no one to meet them at the station, and they found everything unprepared at home. In an absent-minded moment, so the servants told them, the master had left the telegram lying on the table and had gone out, without leaving any instructions. In the evening, when they were already sitting down to eat, they heard the sound of the front door at last. They jumped up and ran to meet him. He looked at them in surprise—obviously he had forgotten the telegram—patiently accepted his daughter's embrace, but without any particular expression of feeling, let them lead him to the dining room and tell him about their journey. However, he asked no questions, smoked his cigar in silence, sometimes answered briefly, sometimes did not notice what they said at all; it was as if he were asleep with his eyes open. Then he got up ponderously and went to his room.

And it was the same for the next few days. His anxious wife tried to get him to talk to her, but in vain; the more she pressed him, the more evasively he reacted. Some place inside him was barred to her, inaccessible, an entrance had been walled up. He still ate with them, sat with them for a while when callers came, but in silence, absorbed in his own thoughts. However, he took no part in their lives any more, and when guests happened to look into his eyes in the middle of a conversation, they had the unpleasant feeling that a dead man's dull and shallow gaze was looking past them.

Even those who hardly knew him soon noticed the increasing oddity of the old man's behaviour. Acquaintances began to nudge each other on the sly if they met him in the street—there went the old man, one of the richest men in the city, slinking along by the wall like a beggar, his hat dented and set at a crooked angle on his head, his coat dusted with cigar ash, reeling in a peculiar way at every step and usually muttering aloud under his breath. If people greeted him, he looked up in surprise; if they addressed him he stared at them vacantly, and forgot to shake hands. At first a number of acquaintances thought he must have gone deaf, and repeated what they had said in louder tones. He was not deaf, but it always took him time to wake himself, as it were, from his internal sleep, and then he would lapse back into a strange state of abstraction in the middle of the conversation. All of a sudden the light would go out of his eyes, he would break off the discussion hastily and stumble on, without noticing the surprise of the person who had spoken to him. He always seemed to have emerged from a dark dream, from a cloudy state of self-absorption; other people, it was obvious, no longer existed for him. He never asked how anyone was; even in his own home he did not notice his wife's gloomy desperation or his daughter's baffled questions. He read no newspapers, listened to no conversations; not a word, not a question penetrated his dull and overcast indifference for a moment. Even what was closest to him became strange. He sometimes went to his office to sign letters. But if his secretary came back an hour later to fetch them, duly signed, he found the old man just as he had left him, lost in reverie over the unread letters and with the same vacant look in his eyes. In the end he himself realised that he was only in the way at the office, and stayed away entirely.

But the strangest and most surprising thing about the old man, to the whole city, was the fact that although he had never been among the most devoutly observant members of its Jewish community he suddenly became pious. Indifferent to all else, often unpunctual at meals and meetings, he never failed to be at the synagogue at the appointed hour. He stood there in his black silk cap, his prayer shawl around his shoulders, always at the same place, where his father once used to stand, rocking his weary head back and forth as he chanted psalms. Here, in the dim light of the room where the words echoed around him, dark and strange, he was most alone with himself. A kind of peace descended on his confused mind here, responding to the darkness in his own breast. However, when prayers were read for the dead, and he saw the families, children and friends of the departed dutifully bowing down and calling on the mercy of God for those who had left this world, his eyes were sometimes clouded. He was the last of his line, and he knew it. No one would say a prayer for him. And so he devoutly murmured the words with the congregation, thinking of himself as one might think of the dead.

Once, late in the evening, he was coming back from wandering the city in a daze, and was halfway home when rain began to fall. As usual, the old man had forgotten his umbrella. There were cabs for hire quite cheaply, entrances to buildings and glazed porches offered shelter from the torrential rain that was soon pouring down, but the strange old man swayed and stumbled on through the wet weather. A puddle collected in the dent in his hat and seeped through, rivulets streamed down from his own dripping sleeves; he took no notice but trudged on, the only person out and about in the deserted street. And so, drenched and dripping, looking more like a tramp than the master of a handsome villa, he reached the entrance of his house just at the moment when a car with its headlights on stopped right beside him, flinging up more muddy water on the inattentive pedestrian. The door swung open, and his wife hastily got out of the brightly lit the interior, followed by some distinguished visitor or other holding an umbrella over her, and then a second man. He drew level with them just outside the door. His wife recognised him and was horrified to see him in such a state, dripping wet, his clothes crumpled, looking like a bundle of something pulled out of the water, and instinctively she turned her eyes away. The old man understood at once—she was ashamed of him in front of her guests. And without emotion or bitterness, he walked a little further as if he were a stranger, to spare her the embarrassment of an introduction, and turned humbly in at the servants' entrance.

From that day on the old man always used the servants' stairs in his own house. He was sure not to meet anyone here, he was in no one's way and no one was in his. He stayed away from meals—an old maidservant brought something to his room. If his wife or daughter tried to get in to speak to him, he would send them away again with a vague murmur that was none the less clearly a refusal to see them. In the end they left him alone, and gradually stopped asking how he was, nor did he enquire after anyone or anything. He sometimes heard music and laughter coming through the walls from the other rooms in the house, which were already strange to him, he heard vehicles pass by until late at night, but he was so indifferent to everything that he did not even look out of the window. What was it to do with him? Only the dog sometimes came up and lay down by his forgotten master's bed.

Nothing hurt in his dead heart now, but the black mole was tunnelling on inside his body, tearing a bloodstained path into quivering flesh. His attacks grew more frequent from week to week, and at last, in agony, he gave way to his doctor's urging to have himself thoroughly examined. The professor looked grave. Carefully preparing the way, he said he thought that at this point an operation was essential. But the old man did not take fright, he only smiled wearily. Thank God, now it was coming to an end. An end to dying, and now came the good part, death. He would not let the doctor say a word to his family, the day was decided, and he made ready. For the last time, he went to his firm (where no one expected to see him any more, and they all looked at him as if he were a stranger), sat down once more in the old black leather chair where he had sat for thirty years, a whole lifetime, for thousands and thousands of hours, told them to bring him a cheque book and made out a cheque. He took it to the rabbi of the synagogue, who was almost frightened by the size of the sum. It was for charitable works and for his grave, he said, and to avoid all thanks he hastily stumbled out, losing his hat, but he did not even bend to pick it up. And so, bareheaded, eyes dull in his wrinkled face, now yellow with sickness, he went on his way, followed by surprised glances, to his parents' grave in the cemetery. There a few idlers gazed at the old man, and were surprised to hear him talk out loud and at length to the mouldering tombstones as if they were human beings. Was he announcing his imminent arrival to them, or asking for their blessing? No one could hear the words, but his lips moved, murmuring, and his shaking head was bowed deeper and deeper in prayer. At the way out of the cemetery beggars, who knew him well by sight, crowded around him. He hastily took all the coins and notes out of his pockets, and had distributed them when a wrinkled old woman limped up, later than the rest, begging for something for herself. In confusion, he searched his pockets, but there was nothing left. However, he still had something strange and heavy on his finger—his gold wedding ring. Some kind of memory came to him—he quickly took it off and gave it to the startled old woman.

And so, impoverished, empty and alone, he went under the surgeon's knife.

When the old man came round from the anaesthetic, the doctors, seeing the dangerous state he was in, called his wife and daughter, now informed of the operation, into the room. With difficulty, his eyes looked out from lids surrounded by blue shadows. "Where am I?" He stared at the strange white room that he had never seen before.

Then, to show him her affection, his daughter leant over his poor sunken face. And suddenly a glimmer of recognition came into the blindly searching eyes. A light, a small one, was kindled in their pupils—that was her, his child, his beloved child, that was his beautiful and tender child Erna! Very, very slowly the bitterly compressed lips relaxed. A smile, a very small smile that had not come to his closed mouth for a long time, cautiously began to show. And shaken by that joy, expressed as it was with such difficulty, she bent closer to kiss her father's bloodless cheeks.

But there it was—the sweet perfume that aroused a memory, or was it his half-numbed brain remembering forgotten moments?—and suddenly a terrible change came over the features that had looked happy only just now. His colourless lips were grimly tightened again, rejecting her. His hand worked its way out from under the blanket, and he tried to raise it as if to push something repellent away, his whole sore body quivering in agitation. "Get away! ... Get away!" he babbled. The words on his pale lips were almost inarticulate, yet clear enough. And so terribly did a look of aversion form on the face of the old man, who could not get away, that the doctor anxiously urged the women to stand aside. "He's delirious," he whispered. "You had better leave him alone now."

As soon as the two women had gone, the distorted features relaxed wearily again into final drowsiness. Breath was still escaping, although more and more stertorously, as he struggled for the heavy air of life. But soon his breast tired of the struggle to drink in that bitter nourishment of humanity. And when the doctor felt for the old man's heart, it had already ceased to hurt him.

THE GOVERNESS

THE TWO CHILDREN are alone in their room. The light has been put out; they are surrounded by darkness except for the faint white shimmer showing where their beds are. They are both breathing so quietly that you might think they were asleep.

One of them speaks up. "I say … " she begins. It is the twelve-year-old, and her voice is quiet, almost anxious in the dark.

"What is it?" asks her sister from the other bed. She is only a year older.

"Good, you're still awake. I … there's something I want to tell you."

No answer from across the room, only a rustle of bed-clothes. The elder sister is sitting up, looking expectant. Her eyes are sparkling.

"Listen … I wanted to ask you … but no, you tell me first, haven't you noticed anything about our Fräulein in the last few days?"

The other girl hesitates, thinking it over. Then she says, "Yes, but I'm not sure what it is. She isn't as strict as usual. I didn't do any school homework for two whole days recently, and she never told me off. And then she's so … oh, I don't know exactly how to put it. I don't think she's bothering about us any more.

She sits somewhere all the time, she doesn't play with us the way she used to."

"I think she's feeling sad, she just doesn't want to show it. She doesn't even play the piano any more."

Silence descends again.

"You wanted to tell me something," the elder girl reminds her sister.

"Yes, but you mustn't tell anyone else, really not anyone, not Mama and not your best friend."

"No, no, I won't!" She is impatient now. "Come on, what is it?"

"Well, when we were going to bed just now, I suddenly remembered that I hadn't said goodnight to Fräulein. I'd taken my shoes off, but I went to her room all the same, ever so quietly, to give her a surprise. And I opened the door of her room very carefully too. I thought at first she wasn't there. There was a light on, but I couldn't see her. Then all at once—it gave me a terrible fright—I heard somebody crying, and I suddenly saw her lying on the bed with all her clothes on and her head in the pillows. She was sobbing so hard that it made me jump. But she didn't notice me. And then I closed the door very quietly again. I had to stand there outside it for a little while because I was trembling so much. And then that sobbing sound came through the door again, quite clearly, and I ran back down here."

The girls keep quiet for a while. Then one of them says, very softly, "Oh, poor Fräulein!" The words linger in the air of the room like a lost, low musical phrase, and then die away again.

"I do wish I knew why she was crying," says the younger sister. "She hasn't quarrelled with anyone these last few days. Mama's leaving her in peace at last instead of scolding her all the time, and I'm sure we haven't done anything bad, not to her. So why was she crying like that?"

"I can think of a reason," says the elder girl.

"What is it? Go on, tell me."

Her sister hesitates, but at last she says, "I think she's in love."

"In love?" The younger girl is baffled. "In love? Who with?"

"Haven't you noticed anything?"

"You don't mean in love with Otto!"

"Oh, don't I? And isn't he in love with her? He's been staying with us for three years while he studies at the university, so why do you think he's suddenly taken to going out with us every day these last few months? Did he ever bother with you or me before Fräulein came to be our governess? He's been hanging around us all the time lately. We keep meeting him by accident in the People's Garden or the City Park or the Prater when we go out with Fräulein. Didn't you notice?"

Startled, the younger girl stammers, "Yes … yes, of course I noticed. Only I always thought it was … "

Her voice fails her. She doesn't go on.

"So did I at first," says her elder sister. "You know how people always say girls are silly. Then I realised that he was only using us as an excuse."

Now they are both silent. It sounds as if the conversation is over. Both girls seem to be deep in thought, or already far away in their dreams.

Then the younger sister breaks the silence in the darkness again. Her voice sounds helpless. "But then why was she crying? He likes her, doesn't he? And I always thought being in love must be wonderful."

"I don't know," says her elder sister, dreamily. "I thought it must be wonderful too."

And once again sleepy lips say, softly and sorrowfully, "Oh, poor Fräulein!"

Then all is quiet in the room.

Next morning they do not discuss the subject again, and yet they are both aware that their thoughts are circling around it. They walk past one another, avoid each other, yet their eyes involuntarily meet when they are glancing surreptitiously at their governess. At mealtimes they watch their cousin Otto as if he were a stranger, although he has been living here with them for years. They do not talk to him, but they keep looking at him from under lowered eyelids to see if he is communicating with Fräulein in some way. Both sisters feel uneasy. They do not play today, and instead do useless, unnecessary things in their nervous anxiety to fathom the mystery. That evening, however, one of them asks the other in a cool tone, as if it were of no importance to her, "Did you notice anything else today?" To which her sister says, "No," and turns away. They are both somehow afraid of talking about it. And so it goes on for a few days, both children silently observing as their minds go round in circles, feeling restlessly and unconsciously close to some sparkling secret.

At last, after a few days, one of them, the younger girl, notices the governess discreetly giving Otto a look full of meaning. He nods in answer. The child quietly takes her sister's hand under the table. When her sister turns to her, she flashes her a meaning glance of her own. The elder girl understands at once, and she too is on the alert.

As soon as they rise from table, the governess tells the girls, "Go to your room and occupy yourselves quietly with something. I have a headache, I'd like to rest for half-an-hour." The children look down. Cautiously, they communicate by touching hands. And as soon as the governess has left, the younger girl hurries over to her sister. "You wait and see—Otto will go to her room now."

"Of course! That's why she sent us to ours."

"We must listen outside her door."

"But suppose someone comes along?"

"Who?"

"Well, Mama."

The younger girl takes fright. "Yes, then … "

"I tell you what. I'll listen at the door, you stay further along the corridor and warn me if there's anyone coming. That way we'll be safe."

The smaller girl looks cross. "But then you won't tell me anything!"

"Yes, I will. I'll tell you all about it."

"Really *all* about it?"

"Yes, I promise. You must cough as a signal if you hear someone coming."

They wait in the corridor, trembling with excitement. Their hearts are beating fast. What will happen? They press close to each other.

Footsteps are approaching. The girls retreat into the shadows. Sure enough, it is Otto. He takes hold of the door handle, and the door closes after him. The elder girl shoots up to it like an arrow from the bow, pressing close to the door, holding her breath as she listens. The younger sister looks wistfully at her from a distance. She is burning with curiosity, and it tears her away from her post. She creeps up, but her sister angrily pushes her away. So she waits at a distance for two or three more minutes that seem to her like an eternity. She is quivering with impatience, stepping from foot to foot as if the floor were burning hot. In her excitement and anger she is near tears—to think that her sister can hear it all and she can't hear anything! Then, in a third room, a door closes. She coughs. And both girls hurry away back to their room. They stand there for a moment breathless, their hearts thudding.

"Come on then, tell me all about it," demands the younger girl avidly.

Her elder sister looks thoughtful. At last she says, dreamily, as if to herself. "I can't make it out!"

"What?"

"It's so strange."

"What? What's so strange?" The younger girl is impatient to know. Her sister tries to collect her thoughts. The smaller girl is pressing very close to her so as not to Fräulein a word.

"It was really funny … not at all what I expected. I think when he came into the room he was going to hug her or kiss her, but then she said, 'Don't do that, I have something serious to discuss with you.' I couldn't see anything, because the key was in the lock on the inside of the door, but I could hear every word. 'Well, what is it?' asked Otto, but I've never heard him speak like that before. You know his usual cheerful, loud way of talking, but he sounded uncertain of himself when he said that, and I felt at once that he was somehow scared. And she must have noticed that he was pretending, too, because she just said very quietly, 'You know what it is.' 'No, I don't, I have no idea,' he said. 'Oh,' she said, so sadly, so terribly sadly, 'then why are you avoiding me

213

all of a sudden? It's a week since you spoke a word to me, you avoid me whenever you can, you don't go out with the children or to the park with us any more. Am I such a stranger all at once? Oh, you know very well why you're keeping away from me.' He said nothing for a bit, then he said, 'I'm about to sit my examinations, I have a great deal of work to do and no time for anything else. It can't be helped.' Then she began crying, and she said to him, through her tears but so kindly, she wasn't angry, 'Otto, why are you lying to me? Tell the truth. I really haven't deserved this from you. I never asked for anything, but now the two of us have to discuss something after all. You know what I am going to say to you, I can see it from your eyes.' And then he said, 'Well, what is it?' But very faintly. And she said … "

Suddenly the girl began trembling, and in her emotion she could get no further. Her younger sister pressed close, saying, "And then what?"

"Then she said, 'What am I going to do about our baby?'"

The smaller girl started with surprise, and cried, "Their baby? What baby? That's not possible!"

"But she said it."

"You can't have heard properly."

"I did, I did. And he repeated it, he sounded just as surprised as you, he cried, 'A baby!' She didn't say anything for quite a time, and then she asked, 'What's to become of me now?' And then … "

"And then?"

"Then you coughed, and I had to run away."

The younger girl stares ahead of her, dismayed. "A baby! But that's impossible. Where *is* the baby?"

"I don't know. That's what I don't understand."

"Maybe at home where … well, where she was living before she came to be our governess. Mama probably wouldn't let her bring the baby with her because of us. And that's why she's so sad."

They both fall silent again, baffled, brooding, unable to come to any conclusions. The thought of the baby is weighing on their minds. Once again it is the smaller girl who speaks first. "A baby, I mean it isn't possible! How can she have a baby? She isn't married, and only married people have babies, I know that!"

"Perhaps she *was* married."

"Don't be so silly. Not to Otto."

"Then how? … "

They stare at each other, at a loss.

"Oh, poor Fräulein," says one of the girls very sadly. They keep repeating the same phrase, and it dies away into a sigh of sympathy. But their curiosity also keeps flaring up.

"I wonder if it's a girl or a boy?"

"How could we find out?"

"Suppose I asked her some time, very, very carefully … What do you think?"

"I think you're crazy!"

"Why? She's so nice to us."

"Oh, do stop and think! No one tells us *that* sort of thing. They hush everything up. When we come into a room they break off their conversation and start talking to us in a silly way as if we were little children. And I'm thirteen already! What's the point of asking? Grown-ups always tell lies."

"But I really, really would like to know."

"Do you think I wouldn't?"

"I tell you what, the bit I understand least is why Otto didn't sound as if he knew about it. You know if you have a baby, the way you know that you have a mother and a father."

"He was only pretending not to know. He's horrid. Otto is always pretending."

"But you wouldn't pretend about something like that. Perhaps he's just trying to fool people … "

However, at this point the governess comes in. They stop talking at once and seem to be doing homework. However, they surreptitiously glance at her. Her eyes look reddened, her voice is rather huskier and more vibrant than usual. The children keep very quiet, suddenly regarding her with awed timidity. She has a baby, they keep thinking, that's why she's so sad. And soon they are feeling sad themselves.

At the dining-room table next day they hear unexpected news. Otto is leaving the family apartment. He has told his uncle that with his examinations so close he has to work very hard, and there are too many distractions here. He will rent a room somewhere for the next month or so, he says, until the exams are over.

The children are very interested to hear this. They guess there is a secret connection with yesterday's conversation, and alert as their instincts now are they pick up the scent of cowardice and flight. When Otto comes to say goodbye to them, they sulk and turn their backs. But they watch surreptitiously as he faces their governess. Her lips are trembling, but she offers him her hand calmly, without a word.

The children have changed a great deal over the last few days. They have lost their playfulness and laughter, the old happy, carefree light has left their eyes. They are full of uneasiness and uncertainty, deeply suspicious of everyone around them. They no longer believe what they are told, they think they detect deliberate lies behind every word. They keep their eyes and ears open all day long, watching every movement, picking up any sudden start of surprise or tone of voice. They haunt the place like shadows in search of clues, listening at doors to overhear anything of interest, possessed by a passionate desire to shake the dark net of secrets off their reluctant shoulders, or at least see through some gap in it and get a glimpse of the real world outside. They have lost their childish trustfulness, their blindly carefree merriment. Moreover, they guess that the tense, sultry atmosphere resulting from recent events will discharge itself in some unexpected way, and they don't want to Fräulein it. Ever since discovering that the people around them are liars they have become persistent and watchful; they are sly and deceitful themselves. With their parents, they take refuge in pretended childishness flaring up into hectic activity. They are a prey to nervous restlessness; their eyes, once shining with a soft, gentle glow, now look deeper and are more likely to flash. In all this constant watching and spying, they feel so helpless that their love for each other is stronger. Sometimes they hug stormily, abandoning themselves to a need for affection suddenly welling up in them, sometimes they burst into tears. All at once, and for no apparent reason, life seems to be in a state of crisis.

Among the many emotional injuries that they now realise they have suffered, there is one that they feel particularly deeply. Seeing how sad Fräulein is these days, they have set out silently, without a word, to please her as much as they possibly can. They do their school exercises carefully and industriously, they help each other, they are quiet and uncomplaining, they try to anticipate her every wish. But Fräulein doesn't even notice, and that hurts them badly. She is entirely different these days. Sometimes, when one of the girls speaks to her, she starts as if woken from sleep. And then her gaze, at first searching, returns from some distant horizon. She will often sit for hours looking dreamily into space, and then the girls go about on tiptoe so as not to disturb her. They have a vague, mysterious idea that she is thinking about her baby who is somewhere far away. And out of the depths of their own awakening femininity they love Fräulein more and more. She is so kind and gentle, her once brisk, high-spirited manner is more thoughtful now, her movements more careful, and the children guess at a secret sadness in all this. They have never seen her shed tears, but her eyelids are often red. They realise that Fräulein is trying to keep her pain secret from them, and are in despair to think that they cannot help her.

And once, when Fräulein has turned to the window and is dabbing her eyes with her handkerchief, the younger girl suddenly plucks up her courage, takes the governess's hand gently, and says, "Fräulein, you're so sad these days. It isn't our fault, is it?"

Much moved, the governess looks at her and caresses her soft hair. "No, my dear, no," she says. "It certainly is not your fault." And she gently kisses the girl's forehead.

It is at this time, when they are keeping watch, letting nothing that moves within their field of vision pass unnoticed, that one of them picks up a remark when she suddenly enters a room. It is only a few words, because the girls' parents break off their conversation at once, but anything they hear now can make them suspicious. "I thought I'd noticed something of that sort myself," their mother was saying. "Well, I'll question her." The child thinks at first that this means her, and almost anxiously runs to her sister for advice and help. But at mid-day they realise that their parents' eyes are resting enquiringly on the governess's dreamy, abstracted face, and then their mother and father look at each other.

After lunch their mother says casually to Fräulein, "Will you come to my room, please? I want to speak to you." Fräulein bows her head slightly. The girls are trembling violently. They can feel that something is brewing.

As soon as the governess goes into their mother's room they hurry after her. This eavesdropping, rummaging about in nooks and crannies, listening and lying in wait has become second nature to them. They are no longer even aware that their conduct is improperly bold and sly, they have just one idea in their heads—to get possession of all the secrets being kept from them. They listen. But all they hear is whispered words, and a soft but angry tone of voice. Their bodies tremble nervously. They are afraid of failing to catch something important.

Then one of the voices inside the room rises higher. It is their mother's. She sounds angry and cantankerous.

"Did you really think everyone's blind, and no one would notice anything? I can well imagine how you've carried out your duties with such ideas in your head, and with morals like that! And it is to such a woman that I have entrusted the upbringing of my children, my daughters, a task that God knows you have neglected ... "

Fräulein seems to be saying something in reply, but too quietly for the children to make out what it is.

"Excuses, excuses! Every promiscuous girl will offer that excuse! She'll blame the first man who comes to mind and think nothing of it, hoping the good Lord will come to her aid. And a woman like that claims to be a governess and fit to educate girls. It's outrageous. You surely don't imagine that, in your condition, I shall keep you in my household any longer?"

The children listen intently outside the door. Shivers run through them. They don't understand what their mother is saying, but it is terrible to hear her voice raised in such anger—and the only answer is their governess's quiet, uncontrollable sobbing. Tears come to their own eyes. But the sobbing only seems to make their mother angrier.

"So all you can do now is burst into tears! You don't touch my heart like that. I have no sympathy for such females. What becomes of you now is none of my business. You'll know where to turn, I'm sure, I'm not asking you for the details. All I know is that I shall not tolerate the presence of someone who has so shamefully neglected her duty in my house a day longer."

221

Only sobs answered her, desperate, wild, animal sobs that shake the children outside the door like a fever. They have never heard anyone cry so hard. And they feel, vaguely, that someone crying like that can't be in the wrong. Their mother is silent now, waiting. Then she says suddenly, brusquely, "Very well, that's all I wanted to say to you. Pack your bags today and come to collect your wages first thing tomorrow. Goodbye."

The children scurry away from the door, and take refuge in their room. What was all that about? They feel as if a bolt of lightning has struck them. Standing there pale and shuddering, for the first time they somehow guess the truth. For the first time, too, they dare to feel hostile to their parents.

"It was wrong of Mama to speak to her like that," says the elder girl, biting her lower lip.

Her younger sister still shrinks from such a bold statement. "But we don't know what she did," she stammers plaintively.

"It can't have been anything bad. Fräulein can't have done anything bad. Mama doesn't know what she's really like."

"And the way she cried—it scared me."

"Yes, it was terrible. So was the way Mama shouted at her. It was wrong of Mama, I tell you it was wrong."

She stamps her foot. Her eyes are blurred with tears. Then the governess comes in, looking very tired.

222

"Children, there are things I have to do this afternoon. You can be left on your own, can't you? I'm sure I can rely on you, and then I'll see you this evening."

She goes out without noticing how upset the children are.

"Did you see her eyes? They were all red with crying. I can't understand how Mama could treat her like that."

"Oh, poor Fräulein!"

That deep, tearful sigh of sympathy again. The children are standing there in distress when their mother comes in to ask if they would like to go for a walk with her. The girls are evasive. They are afraid of their mother. In addition they are indignant; no one has said a word to them about their governess's departure. They would rather be on their own. Like two swallows in a small cage they swoop back and forth, upset by this atmosphere of lies and silence. They wonder whether to go and see Fräulein in her room and ask her questions, talk to her about it all, tell her they want her to stay and Mama is wrong. But they are afraid of hurting her feelings. And they are also ashamed of themselves for having found out all they know on the sly, by dint of eavesdropping. They must pretend to be stupid, as stupid as they were two or three weeks ago. So they spend the long, endless afternoon on their own, brooding over what they have heard and crying, always with those terrible voices ringing in their ears, their mother's vicious, heartless fury and the desperate sobs of their governess.

Fräulein looks in on them fleetingly that evening and says goodnight. The children tremble when they see her going out; they would like to say something to her. But when Fräulein reaches the door she turns back suddenly, as if their silent wish has brought back once more of her own accord. Something is gleaming in her eyes; they are moist and clouded. She hugs both children, who begin sobbing wildly, kisses them once again, and then quickly goes out.

The children are in tears. They sense that she was saying goodbye.

"We won't see her any more!" wails one of the girls.

"No, when we get back from school at mid-day tomorrow she's sure to have gone."

"Maybe we can go and visit her later. And then I'm sure she'll show us her baby."

"Oh yes, she's so nice."

"Oh, poor Fräulein!" It is a sigh for their own loss again.

"Can you imagine what it will be like now without her?"

"I'll never be able to take to another governess."

"Nor me."

"No one else will be so kind to us. And then … "

She dares not say it. But an unconscious sense of femininity has made them revere Fräulein even more since they found out about her baby. They both keep thinking about it, and no longer with mere childish curiosity, but deeply moved and sympathetic.

"Listen," says one of the girls. "I know what!"

"Yes?"

224

"I'd like to do something nice for Fräulein before she goes. So that she'll know we love her and we're not like Mama. What about you?"

"How can you ask?"

"What I thought was, she's always liked white roses so much. Suppose we go out to buy her some first thing tomorrow, before we go to school, and then we can put them in her room."

"But when?"

"At mid-day when we come home."

"She'll be gone by then. I tell you what, suppose I run out very early and buy them before anyone notices I'm gone? And then we can take them to her in her room before we go to school."

"Yes, and we'll get up really early."

They fetch their money boxes, shake out the contents and put all their money together. They feel happier now they know that they can still give Fräulein proof of their silent, devoted love.

They get up very early in the morning. They stand outside the governess's door holding the beautiful double white roses—their hands tremble slightly—but when they knock there is no answer. They think Fräulein must be asleep, and cautiously slip into the room. But it is empty, and the bed has not been slept in. Everything lies scattered around in disorder. A couple of letters in white envelopes lie on the dark tabletop.

The two children take fright. What has happened?

"I'm going to see Mama," says the elder girl with determination. And defiantly, her eyes sombre and entirely fearless, she faces her mother head on and asks, "Where is our Fräulein?"

"She'll be in her room," says her mother, surprised.

"Her room's empty and she hasn't slept in her bed. She must have gone away yesterday evening. Why didn't anyone tell us?"

Her mother doesn't even notice the harsh, challenging tone of the girl's voice. She has turned pale, and goes to see her husband, who quickly disappears into the governess's room.

He stays there for a long time. The child watches her mother, who seems to be upset, with a steady angry gaze that the mother's eyes dare not meet.

Then her father comes back. He is very pale in the face, and is carrying a letter. He goes into the sitting room with her mother and talks to her quietly. The children stand outside, not venturing to listen at the door any more. They are afraid of their father's wrath. Just now he looked as they have never seen him before.

Their mother comes out of the sitting room, her eyes red with tears and appearing distressed. Instinctively, as if attracted to her fear, the children go to meet her, wanting to ask questions. But she says brusquely, "Off you go to school. You're late already."

And the children have to go. As if in a dream they sit there for four or five hours among all the other girls, hearing not a word. They rush home when lessons are over.

Home would be the same as usual except that everyone seems to be in the grip of a terrible idea. No one says anything, but they all, even the servants, look so strange. The children's mother comes to meet them. She seems to have prepared something to tell them. She begins, "Girls, your Fräulein will not be coming back, she has … "

But she does not venture to finish what she was going to say. As her children's eyes meet hers, they flash with such dangerous menace that she dares not tell them a lie. She turns and leaves them, taking refuge in her room.

Otto suddenly turns up that afternoon. He has been summoned; one of the letters left was for him. He too is pale and stands around looking upset. No one speaks to him. They all avoid him. Then he sees the two children huddled together in a corner and goes over to say hello.

"Don't you touch me!" says one of the girls, shuddering with disgust. Her sister actually spits on the floor in front of him. He wanders around for a little longer, looking confused and embarrassed. Then he disappears.

No one talks to the children. They themselves do not exchange a word with anyone. They pace around like caged animals, pale-faced, restless and agitated; they keep coming together, meeting one another's tear-stained gaze, but saying nothing. They know all about it now. They know that they have been told lies, all human beings can be bad and despicable. They do not love their parents any more, they don't believe in them. They know that they can never trust anyone, the whole monstrous weight of life will weigh down on their slender shoulders. They have been cast out of the cheerful comfort of their childhood, as if into an abyss. They cannot quite grasp the terrible nature of what has happened, but the thought of it makes them choke and threatens to stifle them. Their cheeks burn feverishly, and they have an angry, agitated look in their eyes. As if freezing in their isolation, they wander up and down. No one, not even their parents, dares speak to them, they look at everyone with such ill will, and their constant pacing back and forth reflects the agitation working inside them. Although the two girls do not talk to each other about it, they have something dreadful in common. Their impenetrable, unquestioning silence and viciously self-contained pain makes them seem strange and dangerous to everyone. No one comes close to them; access to their minds has been cut off, perhaps for many years to come. Everyone around them feels that they are enemies, and determined enemies at that who will not easily forgive again. For yesterday their childhood came to an end.

That afternoon they grow many years older. And only when they are alone in the darkness of their room in the evening do childish fears surface in them, the fear of loneliness, of images of dead people, as well as a presentiment of indistinct terrors. In the general agitation of the house, no one has remembered to heat the rooms. So they get into one bed together, freezing, holding each other tightly in their thin childish arms, pressing their slender bodies, not yet in the full bloom of youth, close to each other as if seeking help in their fear. They still dare not talk freely. But now the younger girl at last bursts into tears, and her elder sister joins her, sobbing wildly. They weep, closely entwined, warm tears rolling down their faces hesitantly at first, then falling faster, hugging one another breast to breast, shaking as they share their sobs. They are united in pain, a single weeping body in the darkness. They are not crying for the governess now, or for the parents who are lost to them; they are shaken by a sudden horror and fear of the unknown world lying ahead of them, after the first terrifying glimpse that they had of it today. They are afraid of the life ahead of them into which they will now pass, dark and menacing like a gloomy forest through which they must go. Their confused fears become dimmer, almost dreamlike, their sobbing is softer and softer. Their breath mingles gently now, as their tears mingled before. And so at last they fall asleep.

This selection of four novellas by Stefan Zweig contains stories from different periods in his career. The first in the book, *Did He Do It?*, is clearly the last to have been written, although the precise details of its publishing history seem to be uncertain. It is first recorded as appearing in book form in 1987, as part of the collected works of Zweig published by S Fischer, in a volume of several Zweig stories under the general title of *Praterfrühling—Prater Spring*. Internal evidence, however, clearly suggests that this late story must have been written when Zweig was living in Bath just before the outbreak of the Second World War. He had left Austria in 1934, and although he went back for a brief visit later, when the annexation of the country by Nazi Germany was imminent, he did not go to his house in Salzburg, where his first wife and stepdaughters were still living. What seems to have been a fairly amicable divorce followed. Zweig came to live in exile in England, first in London and then in Bath with Lotte Altmann, who was to be his second wife. In his memoir *The World of Yesterday* he describes, with great affection, the city of Bath and the countryside around it in the summer of 1939, when war was brewing. "Such madness," he wrote, "seemed incredible in the face of those meadows flowering on in luxuriant bloom, the peace that the valleys around Bath breathed as if enjoying it themselves." But in early September of that year war came, and Zweig and Lotte, fearing internment as enemy aliens even though he had become a British citizen, swiftly left the country—first for the United States and then for Brazil, where they committed suicide together in February 1942.

The setting of the story in and near Bath, then, places *Did He Do It?* among Zweig's last works, probably post-dated only by the completion of his memoir *The World of Yesterday*, which he had been writing on and off for some time, and his last novella, the famous *Schachnovelle*, often known in English versions as *The Royal Game*, probably written in the autumn of 1941 and published, like the memoir, after his suicide.

Interestingly and rather touchingly, in *Did He Do It?* Zweig is partly emulating the classic English country-house murder mystery, setting a puzzle that involves a probably deliberate killing and the identity of the murderer, even challenging the reader with a title that is a question (in German, *War er es?*—Was it he?). It is also one of several Zweig novellas in which events are narrated through the voice of a woman, in this case Betsy, the wife of a retired colonial official.

The Miracles of Life dates from a much earlier period, and was first published in 1904. Zweig took a great interest in historical subjects, and wrote a number of historical biographies of figures such as Mary Queen of Scots, Marie Antoinette, Magellan and Fouché. Here he imagines the city of Antwerp in 1566, when the Low Countries were still under Spanish rule but beginning to rebel under the Prince of Orange of that time. No date is actually mentioned in the story, but 1566 was the year in which the rioting and iconoclasm in Antwerp that form the background to the novella took place. Zweig, although Jewish, was not an observant Jew. His family had long ago assimilated entirely to the European society of the time, and much later than this story, as Nazi anti-Semitism became rife, Zweig pointed out correctly how much Jews had contributed to the intellectual and cultural lives of many European nations, not least Germany and Austria. But here he presents a sixteenth-century Jewish character who greatly values her lost family background—the girl Esther, rescued from a pogrom by a rough-mannered but good-hearted soldier going home to Antwerp to open an inn. The old painter who is the central character of the story sees her as the perfect model for a painting of the Virgin Mary that he is commissioned to provide as an altarpiece. Devout Christian of his time as he is, he also sees it as his duty to convert her, an idea that horrifies Esther. None the less, genuine friendship develops between the old man and the girl, who tragically dies in a riot when she goes to the cathedral to look at the painting of the baby who modelled with her, and whom she came to love passionately. From a man who was not fervently religious in any way, it is an interesting study of the conflict of two deeply held faiths, and the reconciliation in human terms of the two who represent them. Zweig also had an eye for a detailed historical background, for instance in his account of the cathedral and quayside of Antwerp before the story proper begins.

Another study of Jewish background lies at the core of *Downfall of the Heart*, where the old Jewish business-man who rose from humble origins and worked hard to make a fortune, finds that his wife and daughter do not appreciate his generosity as he thinks they should. In his memoir, Zweig describes, with astonished indigna-tion, the way in which girls when he was growing up in Vienna were deliberately kept in ignorance about both intellectual life (not a proper pursuit for a woman) and sexuality. The old man's daughter Erna, however, is of a later generation; she is a Bright Young Thing of the Twenties, cheerfully flirts with many admirers and, as her father discovers to his horror, is sleeping with one of them. Neither Erna nor her mother behaves well, but the old man's growing rancour and resentment are a grim theme; he withdraws from his family into private brooding and ultimately into the comforts of his traditional religious faith. The strong note of observant Judaism struck at the end is something rarely found in Zweig's work.

The short story *The Governess*, first published in 1911, takes us, however, right back to the prim propriety of Vienna in the early twentieth century as described in *The World of Yesterday*. Zweig mentions an aunt of his own who, on her wedding night, "suddenly appeared back in her parents' apartment at one in the morning," complaining that her new husband "was a madman and a monster. In all seriousness, he had tried to take her clothes off." The aunt must have been seventeen or so at the time, I suppose. What, we may wonder, was her mother thinking of, to keep her in the dark and leave her there? In view of that story, it is not surprising that the two sisters in *The Governess*, aged twelve and thirteen, are entirely ignorant of the facts of life, and are puzzled to hear their governess, of whom they are very fond, telling their student cousin Otto that he and she will have a baby—a baby is "on the way", is the implication of the German expression: literally, "I have a child by you", but the use of the present tense in German makes the girls assume that the baby has already been born. So where *is* the baby? They would love to ask Miss about it. Is it a boy or a girl? But only married people have babies, and their governess is not married! A century later, it is impossible to imagine girls of that age in such a state of ignorance; these sisters, who come to feel that the adult world is set against them, reflect from a feminine point of view the experience of the boy Edgar in *Burning Secret* of 1913, two years later, as he tries to puzzle out the nature of the secret that grown-ups so enviably seem to know.

These four stories are wide-ranging in the diversity of their subjects and the author's approach to them. The least autobiographical of writers in his fiction, Stefan Zweig none the less integrates into it many themes that intrigued his imagination. To read his memoir casts light on many of his stories.

ANTHEA BELL

Other Stefan Zweig titles published by

PUSHKIN PRESS

Amok and Other Stories
Translated by Anthea Bell

Beware of Pity
Translated by Phyllis and Trevor Blewitt

Burning Secret
Translated by Anthea Bell

Casanova
A Study in Self-Portraiture
Translated by Eden and Cedar Paul

Confusion
Translated by Anthea Bell

Fantastic Night and Other Stories
Translated by Anthea Bell

The Royal Game
Translated by Anthea Bell

Twilight
Moonbeam Alley
Translated by Anthea Bell

Wondrak and Other Stories
Translated by Anthea Bell

The World of Yesterday
Translated by Anthea Bell

www.pushkinpress.com